TAKE

ME

HOME

NOW

TAKE ME HOME NOW

The Complete Series Collection

A Gripping Psychological Thriller

OBY ALIGWEKWE

This book is a work of fiction. Characters, names, and events as well as all places, incidents, organizations, and dialog in this novel are either the products of the writer's imagination or are used fictitiously – not portrayed with geographical and historical accuracy.

eISBN: 978-1-7381634-5-8

Cover design by Panagiotis Lampridis

Newsletter Signup: obyaligwekwe.com

To my family

Take Me Home Now
Book One

Chapter One

Hot sweat dripped down Eli's face. His legs, up to his hips, were heavy. His head felt like it belonged to someone who had been dragged for miles by a dozen mules and left for dead. The air was cold, but his body burned as he stared subconsciously into the darkness. A sickly smell, a cross between rusty metal and vinegar, wafted around him. He tried to remember where he was, but his recollection of events from the night before did not match the powerless state he found himself in. Although his heart was pounding heavily in his chest, to him, it felt strangely nonexistent. It was as though his body, from his waist up, belonged to someone else, and everything he'd ever known had vanished.

He slipped in and out of consciousness, and just as he was starting to make sense of his surroundings, two uniformed men barged through the door and headed straight for his bed. His first instinct was to run, but the men subdued him and loaded him onto a stretcher. He woke up in a crowded hospital ward with two tiny windows and a stained ceiling.

"Where am I?" he asked, surprised at the sound of his own voice. He'd been unable to speak before then.

A woman muttered something in Spanish and patted his shoulder to calm him.

"I need…" He started to say and moved his head frantically from side to side before a heavy hand pushed him down while the woman stuck a needle in his arm and sent him back into deep unconsciousness.

———

It'd been six months since the elderly gentleman handed Eli the contest flier in front of the grocery store on his early morning run. Eli wasn't one to fall for hustles, but the man had been too persuasive. He had insisted that Eli take a second look at the grand prize for eight lucky winners, boldly printed on the Dream Voyage contest flier.

"An all-expense-paid trip to Costa Rica for a period agreed upon by the contest promoters and the winners. The

Catch—contestants receive a brand new Q phone reconfigured with an advanced dating app to help them find 'their one true love.'"

His excitement had built as he'd read each word. For as long as he could remember, he'd imagined a new life full of intrigue, adventure, and no Jesse. Without hesitation, Eli entered the contest online, hoping against hope that he would be considered worthy of a miracle by the good man above. Two days later, he received the phone that was promised to all entrants, and from then on, he swiped left and right, day in and day out, until he found Contestant 102. Number 102 had everything going for her. She was beautiful, intelligent, and accomplished, and seemed to accept Eli for all he was.

The selection process was more stringent than he had expected since the rules did not allow contestants to share photos on the app. Each participant rated their perceived level of physical attractiveness using a scale that ranged from one to ten. They also had to support their score by providing details of the physical characteristics that informed their assessment. These included their height, weight, age, skin tone, hair color, and their body measurements. Since accuracy was paramount, the results underwent verification by the contest organizers. Any contestants found fudging the numbers by more than a few points were immediately disqualified.

The dating process was exciting enough to drag Eli out of the hole his lackluster relationship with Jesse had created. He texted 102 daily while Jesse was at work. When she was home, he hid for hours in the bathroom and the garage to engage in his new favorite pastime. He became so enamored with 102 that he began to see the light at the end of the tunnel. In his mind, he'd finally found a way out of his desperate situation.

At the end of the two-month dating period, Eli received a prompt to submit his Q phone to the specified drop box location. He and the other contestants remained under intense scrutiny to ensure no one broke the rules while they waited for the results of the contest. The thought of what losing could entail—never getting the chance to meet 102, coupled with the alternative—spending the rest of his life with Jesse, drove him into depression. It also did not help that the contest rules prohibited the contestants from revealing their true identities to each other, making it impossible for him to contact 102.

Chapter Two

Eli awoke as he did every morning to Jesse's grating tone as she ran around their small two-bedroom townhouse, gathering her things for work. The sound of her voice always infuriated him. Her griping never stopped from the second she woke up to the moment she left for her cold, dingy office on the east end of town.

"I left some coffee on the counter," she said hoarsely. "You better get off your lazy ass and pour yourself a cup before it gets cold."

This statement would always come before a loud bang as she slammed the door to enter the garage. Eli knew this routine all too well. He always waited for the cranking sound of her 1998 Honda as it blasted through the neighborhood and off into the Boston traffic before burying his head under the pillow and squishing it tightly around his ears.

The pounding Eli felt in his head from the whiskey he downed nightly after losing his job was in full effect, but on this particular day, he felt different. For some reason, he'd woken up without the usual sadness he'd felt since that fateful day. He had given four of his best years to Feline Construction, believing that one day he would be lucky enough to be considered for vice president. The owner, Bill Schumacher, had abruptly sold the company out from under his fifteen loyal employees. It had been a year since the new management had interviewed him in Bill's former office and found him wanting. Eli's misguided proclamation that in less than a year, he would rise to the role of a vice president in the company, which he had helped build, had not panned out. He was considered ambitious, and there was fear that he could become a bad influence on the other employees, whom they were desperately struggling to indoctrinate into their new way of thinking.

Eli could not forget the look on Jesse's face that day as he walked through the door with a cardboard box filled with his meager belongings.

"I hope this is not what I think it is," Jesse muttered, tumbling out of the sofa. The air in the dimly lit room was heavy with anticipation as she picked herself up, eyeing the package Eli was carrying. It was a plain, nondescript box, and Jesse couldn't shake the feeling that it held more than met the eye.

"Can you at least wait for me to settle down?" Eli had pleaded, remaining in the doorway of the townhouse, a small space that had become a refuge from the chaos in the outside world. But now, even that sanctuary left him with a sick feeling in the pit of his stomach.

"Why can't you hold down a job?" Jesse had taunted, pouting and shaking her head in disdain as she shifted uncomfortably in her seat, her eyes carrying more than a hint of disappointment.

"Do you want to know what happened or not?" Eli had asked in a monotone.

"Okay. Tell me," Jesse responded, moving to the edge of the seat, preparing to scram at a moment's notice.

"We…Because…" Eli's voice had trailed off. He was exhausted, and Jesse's badgering hadn't helped matters. At that moment, all he wanted to do was step out the door and head anywhere that would keep him as far away as possible from Jesse.

"If only you could read the writing on the wall for once," Jesse had continued, slapping the back of one hand loudly into the other, causing Eli to jump at the sound despite being much bigger than her. "You've wasted so many chances. I know it's not easy to make it in your industry, but you don't help matters by always putting up a challenge once something doesn't go your way."

"Jesee, this was not my fault," Eli said, looking her straight in the eye.

"Whose fault is it then?" she mumbled, yanking her purse from a hanger and stepping out the door before Eli could utter another word.

Eli swallowed hard, his shoulders slumping with the weight of acceptance yet horrified by what he felt was heartlessness on Jesse's part. He remained standing for a few minutes, the box still in his hands, unable to move or open his mouth to speak. It was true he had never made it past the first-year mark at all the other jobs he held since he met Jesse ten years prior, but this instance was different. He had been entirely dedicated and had been able to keep it for four years. In his mind, he deserved more credit than Jesse was willing to give him, but he never got the chance to explain.

The pain of her actions was palpable, and he needed a strategy to regain some of his power. Giving Jesse the cold shoulder was the only way Eli knew to punish her. This approach certainly helped him even the score because, above everything else, Jesse hated being ignored.

With the silent treatment in place, Eli entered his "early retirement," as he termed it, in peace, free from Jesse's control, but this lasted only a few days. His need for intimacy had led him to break the ice between them, further worsening his situation. Jesse cursed him out at every opportunity. She even demanded that he keep track of his daily activities and report to her at the end of each day to ensure he made the best use of his time while she was away. Life became so intolerable for him that he couldn't imagine how he could survive another day with her. He desperately needed something, one that would turn his situation around, and soon.

Eli had begun to lose hope of ever meeting 102 when his cell phone rang while he was about to doze off after Jesse left for work in her Honda. He scrambled out of bed to pick up the phone from where he had left it on top of a pile of clothes during his late-night binge.

"Hello!" he answered, his chest heaving in excitement as he waited for the caller to speak.

"I'm from Tidal Tours. I hope we didn't get you at a bad time," the high-pitched female voice on the other side said after pausing for a second.

"Did you say Tidal Tours?" Eli answered.

"Yes. I'm an agent of the company. Is this a good time to speak?"

"Absolutely! I've been expecting your call for months now. Please go on… Continue!"

"First, we need to confirm a few things. Are you Eli… Dubrowsky?"

"Yes! This is Eli," he said, now unable to contain himself.

"What is your contestant ID," she said tersely.

"Erm…101."

"Everything checks out with the information we have on file. One more thing. Can you please confirm the contestant ID for your match? I promise that will be the final verification step before I tell you why I called you this morning."

"That's easy. 102," Eli blurted out like a fourth grader with an axe to grind.

"Thank you. That also checks out. We're calling to inform you that you've been selected as one of the winners in the 'Dream Voyage' contest. From the thousands of entries we received, we have selected eight winners for the grand prize, and you're one of the lucky ones. Now, we'll need a few things from you to process things on our end and get you on your way to enjoy your win."

Eli gasped and shook his head. "Can you repeat what you just said?" he pleaded.

"I said that you're one of the winners of our grand prize in the 'Dream Voyage' contest," the caller repeated slowly.

Eli was frozen to the spot, unable to speak, move, or even swat the fruit fly that was about to perch on his nose. He stood there with the phone in his hand for several long seconds after the caller finished speaking. His life had become so unbearable that he couldn't believe his luck. He'd stopped dreaming, so he couldn't imagine something this good could come his way.

"Hello…Are you there?" the agent asked, rousing Eli from his reverie.

"I'm so sorry. I needed a moment to digest this information," he responded, "I wanted to be sure I heard you right."

"I believe I was clear enough," the agent responded with a chuckle.

Eli shook his head fiercely and blinked twice to make sure he was not dreaming. It took him another moment to fully regain his senses. He then glanced around the untidy room as many thoughts flew through his mind, Contestant 102 being chief among them. "This is the best news I've heard in a long time!" he exclaimed, jumping on the spot. As his thoughts drifted to Jesse, he screeched "This will teach her a lesson…" at the top of his voice.

"Pardon me?" the caller asked in a flustered tone.

"Sorry. I didn't mean for you to hear that," he apologized after realizing he had vocalized his deepest, darkest thoughts to another person. He'd been waiting for an escape for so long. Finally, his chance had come. "Where do we go from here?"

"We have some contracts for you to sign at our office this afternoon. You will be required to leave within the next three weeks, but the exact date of your travel will be entirely up to you."

"What time do you need me there?" he asked expectantly.

"Any time after noon. Bring along two pieces of ID and your passport. I have sent our address to your email."

"Thank you," Eli responded as the phone call ended with a click. He was now fully awake, and his initial shock was wearing off and was being replaced by unfathomable joy.

Still in his night clothes, he waltzed through the rooms in the house, singing a tune he remembered from childhood. Occasionally, he'd stop and pinch himself to confirm all this was really happening to him. He threw on his bathrobe and stepped outside the townhouse to pick up the morning papers but immediately ran back when a blast of February wind hit his face. It was still a couple of hours till noon, so he poured himself a cup of coffee and grimaced as he walked past the dirty kitchen sink. Dishes and leftovers from last night's dinner littered the counter.

He growled in disgust as he stepped on a piece of fruit and almost toppled to the ground. "I'll be damned if I touch any of this," he muttered under his breath. He was about to be free from chores and all his other responsibilities, and he felt truly liberated for the first time in his life.

After a quick shower, he draped one of his good suits over the sofa and then took his phone to call Jesse. On the third ring, Eli heard her weary voice. "Hello, hello. Can I call you back? I'm heading out to an important meeting. Have you cleaned the kitchen from last night's dinner?"

"What the heck are you asking me?" Eli shouted. "Have I cleaned the kitchen? Am I your maid? For once, can you try cleaning it yourself? Besides, I also have an important meeting to attend this afternoon."

"What meeting? A job interview?" Jesse squealed, ignoring his outburst.

"No. Not for a silly job," Eli responded, scoffing at the excitement in her voice. He was so happy to disappoint her and resented her even more for her one-track mind.

"What is it for then?" Jesse asked after a brief silence.

"The topic is too heavy for the phone. I should wait till you get home."

"Try me."

"Well…It's about a contest I entered about six months ago."

"Okay? Did you win?" Jesse asked impatiently.

"I was—"

"Oh my God!" Jesse exclaimed before he could finish his sentence. "I'm so sorry, Eli. I'm almost late for my meeting. Can we discuss this when I get home? I really do have to go now," she pleaded and hurriedly hung up the phone.

Eli's jaw dropped as he stared at the phone in astonishment, muttering something under his breath before hanging up and dressing up to leave.

Chapter Three

At Tidal Tours, Eli took the elevator to the fortieth floor, the topmost in the building. As he entered the reception, he was greeted by a petite woman in a clean-cut navy blue skirt suit with stiletto boots. The woman's face lit up with a smile as she approached him.

"I'm Felicia, your tour representative," she said with her hands outstretched. "How are you doing? I hope it wasn't too hard for you to find us."

"I'm doing extremely well. Your office was a bit out of my way, but not a problem," Eli mumbled as he shook her hand and deliriously thought about Contestant 102.

"Well. I'm glad you made it on time. Do you have your passport or driver's license? Either one of them will do for now."

"Here's my driver's license," Eli replied, handing it to her.

She took one look at the plastic and then at Eli. "Come with me. There's lots of paperwork to go over in my office," she said, leading the way.

They passed a row of cubicles and a corridor with massive glass windows that provided breathtaking views of Boston's financial district. Its sleek condos and stately banks were exquisitely designed, each one more imposing than the next. When they arrived at Felicia's office, she closed the door behind them and ushered him to a seat before taking another seat across from him.

"Congratulations again!" she said, sweeping her sand-colored hair to one side and giving him a long stare. "You're one lucky guy."

"I know," Eli said with a twisted smile. "I never considered myself lucky before now. I guess there's always a first time for everything. Thank you and your team for making this happen."

"The contest was so popular," Felicia continued. "There were so many entries. In fact, thousands of them. At some point, we considered increasing the number of winners, but the sponsors changed their minds at the last minute. You must be thrilled!"

"I am! Extremely! And this couldn't have come at a better time. My daily life is so monotonous that I was going crazy sitting in my apartment day after day catering to Jesse's needs at the expense of mine. That is about to change. You've no idea what this will do for me. I'll forever be grateful."

"Well," said Felicia, tilting her head to one side, "let's get down to brass tacks. Here's the contract we need you to sign. Take your time to read it carefully because the terms are irrevocable. If you want, you can call your lawyer to take a look, but whatever the case, you must hand it in today or the offer is off the table."

"I don't have a lawyer. I didn't think I'd need one."

"Well, you don't really need one," she said, her voice cutting over his. "Some people like a lawyer to look over every contract they receive before signing. This one is pretty straightforward, in my opinion."

As she spoke, Eli scanned the pages of the contract and did not find clauses that would justify hiring a lawyer and risking late submission. At intervals, his mind flew to Jesse. He knew what she would expect him to do in that circumstance, so he was determined to do the opposite.

"I'll be fine," Eli finally said to Felicia, grinning at the thoughts that were flying around in his head.

"In that case, I presume you'll be ready to submit it to me at the end of the hour. Good luck to you!" Felicia said, handing Eli a pen.

"Thank you. I'll do my best to get it done on time."

"Remember to select the duration of your stay—at least three months. Oh, and pay attention to that section there," she said, pointing at the fine print. "Come with me. I've got a comfortable desk for you to work out of."

She got up and stepped out of the room with Eli trailing behind her. Two doors down, she stopped to usher him in. As she swept her hair away from her neck in slow motion, Eli spotted a tattoo of an echoing heart at the nape of her neck. It was an interesting color, a shade between purple and red. A black arrow with a golden point was shooting out of the left side of the tattoo.

Eli wanted to say, "Nice ink," but instead, he said, "Excuse me, what about the other contestants?"

"What about them?"

"Do I get to meet them before the trip?"

"I'm not sure what you mean. Each contestant will have to sign their contract independently of the others. A different department handles the details of when and how you meet. I'm not privy to such information."

"Sorry, I didn't mean it to sound like an interrogation," Eli pleaded. "I'm honestly still trying to recover from my shock and make sense of all of this."

"No need for apologies," Felicia said waving her hands. "I'll excuse myself now so you can get started."

Eli got to work the moment she left, reviewing the terms of his contract. Most of it seemed to be mere formalities. He ticked the box for an extended stay and buzzed Felicia forty-five minutes into the hour.

"That was fast!" exclaimed Felicia when she entered the room and found Eli sitting with his arms crossed over his chest.

"Nothing I haven't seen before," he joked.

"Okay!" Felicia said with a smirk. "Thank you so much for stopping by. We'll call you tomorrow to finalize arrangements."

Eli was elated by the thought of his coming adventure. Outside, a slight rain had replaced the snow, which made the air unusually fresh. He stopped for a moment to admire the building's architecture. He had missed the chance earlier as he rushed to make it inside on time. Just then, it dawned on him that the structure was more magnificent than he'd thought when he arrived that afternoon—imposing architecture, with a twin tower overlooking the harbor. He was thrilled and at peace. Everything was finally working in his favor.

On getting to his car, he gasped as he saw the ticket on his windscreen. "This is ridiculous! Don't tell me I overstayed my welcome," he muttered under his breath as he reviewed the information on the piece of paper. For the first time since he arrived that afternoon, he noticed the road sign that read, "Parking prohibited after three o'clock." He had missed this in his excitement. *I will be long gone before the bill comes in the mail,* he thought, convincing himself that Jesse would take care of this inconvenience the same way she took care of everything else. With that thought playing in his mind, he shredded the ticket, cast the pieces into the air, and watched the shards settle in different corners of the street.

Smiling triumphantly, he headed into the Boston traffic during rush hour and stopped at the coffee shop near his house. It was five o'clock by the time he arrived. The rain had stopped, and a dark cloud now covered the sky, casting a gloomy atmosphere around the plaza and threatening to ruin his happy mood. Not one for small talk, he found a remote corner in the parking lot and took a moment to check the other cars to make sure none belonged to any of his or Jesse's friends. Jesse usually got back from work every day around six o'clock. If he stayed out long enough to get home after her, that would annoy the living daylights out of her and satisfy his craving to punish her. With time to spare, he slowly sipped on his coffee and flipped through the pages of a magazine he'd picked from a stand at the entrance. At intervals, he thought about 102 and hissed audibly as his mind wandered back to his conversation with Jesse that afternoon. *How dare she ask me if I cleaned the sink when I was calling to gloat?* Eli thought and then chuckled to himself.

Chapter Four

Eli could not remember when his resentment for Jesse began. They had attended high school together but were never involved romantically. Five years after graduation, they met again at a mutual friend's wedding. Eli had been painfully shy even with his striking good looks, tall, handsome, and muscular. He had been a star player on his high school's football team, but his achievements had been below the expectations his family and friends had set for him. That had eroded his confidence and was apparent in everything he did—the jobs he accepted, his friendships, and how he spoke about himself.

Jesse, on the other hand, radiated confidence and excelled at everything she put her mind to. When they met, she was still reeling from the breakup with her ex and was not emotionally stable enough to handle a new relationship. She had agreed to dinner on a whim when Eli called to ask her several days later. Jesse had walked into the crowded restaurant wearing a blue mid-length Herve Leger dress. Pointy-toed maroon-red pumps, with little bows at the ankle, adorned her feet. Eli had stared at her full, pouty lips whenever she spoke. Each time she turned to remove layers of dark silky hair from her face and shoulders and her full breasts bounced, his throat constricted. His Adam's apple bulged as he swallowed hard. Any onlooker could see he was awestruck by her. They went out a few more times and eventually got accustomed to each other, arranging a marriage ceremony in Bora Bora later that year.

Eli loved Jesse but was never sure that she loved him in return. That she laughed at most of his jokes was enough for him. He was content with their arrangement and their closeness in those early days. As the years passed, they drifted apart, blaming it on the pressures of life. At some point, Eli's feelings towards her shifted from admiration to animosity. He despised how she spoke to him, looked down on him, and even how her success made him feel. Her job as a manager at the department store provided her with more opportunities than he could ever dream of. It also stole her time away from the family, forcing him to take on the caretaker role for the household. He hated this role, especially as Jesse took every chance she got to remind him that he ought to pull his weight around the house. They argued fiercely at times, drawing the attention of neighbors when things got too heated. On her part, Jesse buried herself in her work to escape the hostility. Eli simply waited for his lot to change.

Both of them had agreed they didn't want children. Eli didn't like children. He didn't want to be burdened with the responsibility. Being an only child, he was used to getting all the attention he needed from his parents. Jesse was indifferent, and since her relationship with Eli was dreary, she didn't want to further complicate matters by bringing kids into the mix. She had thought about leaving him several times in their ten-year marriage, but her busy life dictated how much time she had to spare on anything other than work. Since they dared not confess their feelings to each other, they lived in complete misery. But the prize was Eli's escape.

Jesse was nowhere to be found after Eli got home at ten that evening. This infuriated him. Yet again, he would be home, and she would return long after traffic had returned to normal. She would walk in with that same air of importance that she carried with her every day, holding her shoulders high as the sole breadwinner in their home. He always wanted to put her in her place whenever she asked, "Anything for dinner?" in her haughty voice.

As he settled in front of the television to watch his lineup of Wednesday shows, Jesse walked through the door with a brown paper bag under her arm. Eli recognized takeout from the Chinese restaurant on Washington Street.

"Hey. You hungry? I got us something to eat," Jesse announced in a sing-song voice, eyeing Eli surreptitiously.

"Nope!" answered Eli with an air of indifference. "I'm good."

"You sure? It's Chinese. Sure you don't feel like having?" Jesse responded miserably as she placed the bag on the dining table.

For a second, Eli felt like a jerk for picking a fight in his head when Jesse was out picking up food for both of them, but he still knew to brace himself as there was no telling when her niceness would wear off and be replaced by Jesse being Jesse again. Besides, there was still the matter of informing her about his trip without giving away any of the juicy details. The pleasure he'd felt earlier from knowing how much the news would affect her slowly dissipated as she chattered excitedly around the house while she set the table for the two of them. He still needed to give her the news but no longer had interest in hurting her.

"Are you having any or not?" Jesse continued to persuade Eli, jolting him from his reverie.

"It smells good. Okay, I'll have some," Eli said, rising to join Jesse at the table. "There's always room for Chinese."

"Can you grab a serving spoon from the kitchen?" Jesse pleaded absentmindedly as she removed steaming bowls of wonton soup and chicken fried rice from the bag and placed them on the dining table.

Her request did not go well with Eli as he immediately collapsed onto the sofa, shaking his head from side to side. "Wow!" he exclaimed. "A leopard…or should I say leopardess never really changes her spots. Grab the spoon by yourself, Jesse. Why do you derive so much joy in bossing me around? For once in your life, have some respect!"

Stunned by Eli's reaction to what she imagined was a simple request, Jesee's mouth flew open. "What on earth is wrong with you?" she shrieked. "By the way, I'll act with respect when you start acting like the man around here."

"I will, ma'am," Eli responded sarcastically before turning off the television and gathering his things to leave. "Before you know it, I'll be out of your hair, and I'll be so far away from you, it'll be impossible for me to come home even if there's an emergency. Very soon, and I mean really soon, you won't have to worry about my sitting on your couch all day, eating your crappy food."

The whole time Eli was berating her, Jesse acted unbothered, rolling her eyes, slowly chewing her food, and shaking her head at intervals until he made that proclamation about emergencies. That hit a nerve, prompting her to stand abruptly, almost tipping the table over. "Does this have something to do with the contest you told me about earlier?" she hissed. "So, you won? Congratulations!" she continued, thrusting her neck forward like an alligator as she clapped her hands in derision.

"You can keep your compliments," Eli jeered. "I do not need it."

Jesse had expected that Eli would be frustrated after two years without a job, but what she didn't realize was how resentful their current arrangement had made him. His outburst had killed her appetite and made it hard for her to remain in his presence, so she silently packed the dishes on the table and carried them to the kitchen sink.

"I'm actually happy for you Eli," she finally mustered the strength to say after she returned to grab her drink from the table.

"You don't sound that happy," he retorted. "You'll be stunned by how much things are going to change around here," he said, crinkling his nose.

"Enlighten me," Jesse said, fluttering her lashes, but he ignored her and stormed in the direction of the bedroom. That incensed her. "Is that why you entered the contest? To stun me? To get away from me? I didn't realize I had become such an unbearable presence in your life. Do whatever blows your balloon, Eli," Jesse screamed, making up a new phrase on the fly. "I don't care one bit. Soon, you'll come running back, looking for a shoulder to cry on," Jesse concluded mockingly.

Many nights, Jesse had returned home to find Eli wallowing in self-pity. Their small argument had left her exhausted and confused and unable to think. Resigning herself to another evening of loneliness, she waited until she could no longer hear his footsteps before she entered the kitchen to grab a bowl of ice cream. Sitting in front of the television with her legs on the center table, she heaped large portions of the ice cream into her mouth as she watched an episode of *"The Bachelorette."*

Chapter Five

An hour later, Jesse walked into the bedroom, hoping Eli was asleep so she could settle down for the night without incident, but she found him sitting on the bed with his head in his hands. He looked up when he heard her come in, a forlorn look spreading across his face as he got up and walked towards her to try and make amends. Jesse walked back and forth, pretending to be desperately searching for something, ignoring him as he tried to take her in his arms.

"I'm sorry for how I reacted," Eli said, staring into her face after he managed to stop her by placing both hands firmly on her shoulders.

"I'm sorry too. I should not have spoken to you the way I did," Jesse said after she'd hesitated for a second.

"Does that mean you've forgiven me?" he asked, staring deep into her eyes.

"Yeah. Sure. I've already forgotten about it," Jesse lied, slowly removing his hands so she could carry on with her nightly routine. "I need to get ready for sleep."

"Ok dear," Eli responded, heading to the bed while Jesse peeled off her clothes, littering the floor as she walked to the bathroom. Despite their differences, Eli still had feelings for her. His resentment towards her was mostly out of their issues. To him, if those issues disappeared, they could still have a fighting chance. His heart beat faster as he clicked on the remote until he found something appropriate for the mood while he waited for her to return. Some minutes later, she walked into the room with a towel around her chest and another arranged like a turban on her hair. A few ringlets escaped and dripped water slowly down her shoulder, disappearing into her cleavage. Eli looked on with longing as she put on a silk red negligee with lace cutouts and a matching robe before stopping at the vanity table to apply lotion to her hands and legs.

"Do you need help with your back?" he asked, his throat constricting.

"No thanks. I'm fine," Jesse muttered.

"I haven't seen you wear that in ages," Eli teased, placing the remote on the bedside as she made her way to the bed. He cleared his throat and leaned towards her after she slipped under the sheets.

"Where have you been hiding this?" he whispered seductively into her ear.

"What?" she asked, eyeing him surreptitiously.

"The red number."

"Well…All my PJs are dirty, and I couldn't find anything else to wear," Jesse replied. She was trying to seem indifferent but ended up sounding sultry.

"I was hoping you put that on for me," Eli teased, drawing out his words.

"Not a chance," Jesse retorted.

His face crinkled in a smile. "Not even a little bit?"

"What do you want to hear?" she said, softly touching the side of his face. His pleading tone could only mean one thing, and she could not ignore her own needs any longer. Their quarrel had almost thrown a wrench in her plans, but the red negligee had put them back on track.

"Come to me," Eli said, pulling her towards him.

She curled into him and stared into his eyes, which had turned one shade darker than its usual brown hue. Placing a hand over her waist, Eli turned her onto her back in one swift motion, skillfully peeling the clothes off her shoulders and away from her hips.

"Easy Eli," Jesse cooed.

"Do you know how long I've been waiting for this?" he responded, running his hands along her curves.

For a moment, she resisted. Then, without notice, she dug her knees into his chest, sending his back onto the bed before sliding on top of him like melting ice cream. Eli gasped as she planted a lingering kiss on his lips. He loved it when she took charge in the bedroom but not so much in the other rooms. Starved for intimacy, they went at each other like wild animals before she collapsed into his arms. For as long as their passion lasted, they traveled to a different world, entirely of their own, devoid of the issues that rocked their marital life. Their lovemaking was both an expression of the pain represented by the power tussle that had characterized their relationship from the beginning and the resulting triumph from a mesmerizing meeting of their minds.

"That was amazing," Eli chirped as he watched Jesse untangle her hair after she slid away from him and assumed her position on the bed.

"I haven't heard you say that in a long time. At least not to me," Jesse complained. "Now you're going away. How long will you be gone?"

"Three months."

"Three whole months?" she said in a distressed tone.

"Yeah! Sorry, I should have discussed it with you before committing," he lied. He was angry with her for spoiling the mood.

"Yes, you should have, although I doubt that would have made any difference. When do you leave?"

"In two days," he said, scratching his head.

"Two days?" she screamed. "C'mon, Eli. You can't leave for three months in two days."

This was the pattern in their relationship. Friends one day, and the next day, they were at each other's throats. It was mind-boggling how explosive their bond was.

Eli could already sense something was brewing, so he thought carefully about what he wanted to say next to avoid another huge fight just days before his trip.

"I tried to tell you when I called your office, but you never gave me the chance to speak. I waited for you to return my call, and when I didn't hear from you, I went ahead and signed the contract."

"There was a contract?" Her eyes were wide open.

"Yes. I had to sign one."

"So where is it? Can I see it?" Jesse demanded, jumping out of bed and throwing on her robe. "Where's your copy?"

"Why do I need a copy?" Eli asked, shaking his head derisively. "I don't have any. I submitted it to the company."

"Why do you need a copy?" Jesse repeated, staring at him in disbelief. First of all, how can you sign a contract without having a lawyer or anyone review it? Also, without your own copy, how can you prove what you signed? You're crazy!"

"Enough! Stop insulting me," Eli cautioned.

"You do this all the time," Jesse continued, ignoring his warning. "You make crazy decisions and expect me not to voice my opinion. That's insane!"

"I said enough!" Eli was now screaming at the top of his voice. As Jesse looked on, he grabbed a pillow and walked out of the room to spend the night on the sofa like he had done so many times in their marriage.

Alone with his thoughts, Eli pondered the possibility of never returning to Jesse and smiled. "Serves her right," he muttered under his breath.

Just then, it occurred to him that he had not told her where he was going but decided to do so before she left for work the next day, hoping that would deliver the right punch.

He found himself in an unusual situation. He had never been a creature of routine, the kind that stuck to the familiar and predictable. But his next plan of action was at a different level. As he lay on the sofa, the soft glow of the dying street lamp casting a warm ambiance, his mind was consumed by a familiar thought—what his connection with Contestant 102 would end up looking like. Would she share his interests, his dreams, or perhaps even his fears? He pondered whether their worlds would collide in beautiful harmony or clash like discordant notes in a symphony. The anonymity of numbers gave him the freedom to imagine a connection beyond the constraints of societal norms.

Before he dozed off, Eli wondered what being with 102 would feel like, how she would smell, and how she would taste. The more he thought of her, the faster his heart thumped, and with each thump, his impatience grew, and soon, he started counting the hours leading to the time he could have 102 there with him.

Chapter Six

Two days later, Eli boarded the Costa Airways flight to Costa Rica. Though he was excited to be on an all-expense paid trip, he said goodbye to Jesse that morning with mixed feelings. As far as he was concerned, their relationship was irredeemable. He felt sad about the state of his family life. When and if he ever returned, he planned to ask her for a divorce so they could both get a second chance at love.

Eli barely got any sleep from his first-class cabin as he fantasized about 102 the entire flight. When the plane landed at five PM local time, he wasted no time heading towards customs. The faster he could get to 102, the sooner he could start this much-anticipated phase of his life. A Tidal Tours employee, a tall man in his late twenties wearing a face cap, welcomed him right outside the baggage claim area, handing Eli several pamphlets and a gift bag.

"I'm Ty, your tour agent from Tidal Tours. Welcome to Costa Rica," Ty said with a firm handshake. "I'll be available to answer all your questions from now on. How was your flight?"

"It was everything I imagined," Eli said, nodding. "Thank you very much."

He perused the pamphlets one after the other and marveled at the amount of adventure promised on every single page.

"A driver is waiting to take you to your accommodation — a luxury studio apartment by Conchal Beach," Ty said as they walked past the crowd of travelers and through the sliding doors where a fleet of cars was waiting.

He beckoned to a black limousine, which pulled up right beside them. After they had settled into the back seat, Ty pulled out a bottle of champagne, poured it into two tall glasses, and handed one to Eli.

From the way Eli twitched in his seat the entire ride, Ty could tell he couldn't wait to start his adventure.

"Hey man," Ty said thirty minutes later, distracting Eli as he took in the perfect view of the lush landscape and the beautiful sky, which had begun to turn orange as the sun was disappearing on the horizon. "The pamphlets I gave you include details of all the activities we have arranged for you. There's also an unending list of what you can do with your time outside of the activities we have selected. However, I doubt you'll ever find the time to explore on your own. Here we are…"

He paused when the driver pulled into a picturesque apartment complex with beautiful fountains, a swimming pool, and a tennis court in the far corner. The tropical breeze was a welcome change, as it caressed his skin and brought a sense of relaxation and comfort. A hard beat hit Eli's heart as he admired the surroundings. He couldn't believe how beautiful everything looked, but one thing was top of his mind. "Where…When will I meet 102?" he asked unashamedly.

"Tomorrow. She'll be arriving tomorrow."

"Great!" Eli's face lit up with a smile. His life was now perfect.

"I'll accompany you to your room and let you settle in. You're at complete liberty to set your own schedule today. Here's my number," Ty said, handing Eli a business card with his number typed in bold letters. "Call me if you need anything. Okay?"

"I sure will. Thanks, Ty."

Immediately after Ty left, Eli opened the fridge, took out a can of beer, cracked it open, and gulped everything down in one motion. The golden sun peeked through the linen drapes. He pushed them apart to reveal the full view of the ocean before peeling off his clothes and walking to the bathroom. As he was about to enter the shower, he heard a beeping sound that seemed to pause right after it started. Making nothing of the disturbance at first, he convinced himself as he took a long bath that the sound had come from one of the apps on his phone. After his bath, he picked up his phone while he wiped his body with a towel. It was then that he realized the phone had been off for hours since he entered the plane in Boston. He had turned the phone off on the flight and in his excitement had forgotten to turn it back on after the plane landed.

He glanced around the room to see if he could identify anything else that could point him in the direction of the sound, later giving up when he got distracted by the sound of party music in the distance. He settled down to eat his dinner, which was already waiting on his desk when he entered the room. Just as he was about to heap a spoonful of food into his mouth, the beep sounded again, followed by a light buzz like the quenching of a generator.

"Hell no!" Eli exclaimed, abandoning his meal.

He gasped in astonishment and waited for everything to die down before pulling up the mattress to search under the bed for clues, but he found none. Now that he had eliminated his phone as the culprit, he searched all corners of the room, hoping to identify the source of the noise. After five minutes of tearing up everything, from the bedcovers to the rug, and the colorful pillow arrangement on the chaise lounge by the window, he decided to give up on his search and call Ty. He dismissed that thought the second it crossed his mind. He could not afford to become entangled in anything that could disrupt his mission in Costa Rica. In his mind, if the contest organizers received a complaint from him barely one hour after they set him up in these beautiful surroundings, they could label him ungrateful, which could be grounds for terminating his contract. He weighed the pros and cons of alerting Ty and later decided the beeping sound was nothing, only a minor inconvenience.

Chapter Seven

Eli slept peacefully that night, despite the absurd events that had taken place since his arrival at the apartment. The bed was lush and comfortable, providing a much-needed respite from the chaos of the day. The air in the room was cool and refreshing, a welcome change from the cold, crisp winter days Eli was used to in Boston. The combination of the two created a unique and enjoyable experience, making him feel pampered and rejuvenated. He was able to drift off into a peaceful slumber, feeling grateful for the comfort and tranquility of his new surroundings. It was a stark contrast to his previous living situation, and he couldn't help but feel grateful for the upgrade.

He always credited himself to being a dreamer, but until that night, Contestant 102 had never appeared to him in a dream. In the dream, they were running hand in hand towards a tall building, laughing and enjoying each other's company. They would stop along the way to share kisses and gaze into each other's eyes. The air was filled with a refreshing and clean scent, reminiscent of the aftermath of a heavy rain. It was a dream that felt exhilarating and full of joy. She was everything he'd imagined. All her parts and pieces had been just as she had described herself on the Q phone during the dating process, with no embellishments, no disappointment. He couldn't believe his luck in finding someone who was exactly what he had been looking for.

Eli's heart was racing when he woke up, trying to make sense of what he had just experienced. It had felt so vivid, so real, that when he found himself alone on the bed, clutching the blanket tightly as though it were a person, it suddenly dawned on him that he had lost all capability of distinguishing between illusion and reality. The only evidence left of his outer worldly experience was his boner and the crooked grin on his face, leaving him feeling disoriented and unsure. Deep down, he couldn't help but hope that maybe, just maybe, his dream was more than a glimpse of what could be in his future.

The clock on his bedside table said eight, and with only thirty minutes left before Contestant 102 was scheduled to arrive, Eli jumped out of bed and rushed into the bathroom. He stared at his naked body across the bathroom mirror and grinned as some of the nervousness he felt at that moment quickly disappeared. What he saw assured him that he had what it took to seduce any woman, let alone 102 who he believed had fallen hook, line, and sinker for him during the dating period. After the obligatory shower and a quick shave, he put on a pair of dark blue jeans and threw a navy blue shirt over a white t-shirt. "I will charm her to bits," he said out loud, an attempt to assure himself that he would handle 102's arrival with ease, but in his mind, he was thinking, *what if she takes one look and runs for the door?*

As the minutes ticked by, Eli could feel his heart racing with anticipation. It seemed like time was moving at a snail's pace. Unable to contain his nerves, he began pacing around the room, his mind filled with excitement. Finally, at exactly half past eight, he heard a soft tapping against the door. It was a delicious sound, one that could only mean one thing—that 102 had arrived. Had Eli been less athletic, he most definitely would have pulled a muscle with the way he ran to the door.

It was the red shoes he noticed first, pointy at the toes, with little bows at the ankle. His eyes traveled up the familiar legs to the hips he had come to know after so many years and rested on her face. Tiny wisps of hair jostled to set themselves free from a tightly held bun, and those eyes that had taunted and tortured him in the past now welcomed and pleaded. Surely, his eyes were deceiving him.

His eyes must have been deceiving him.

Take Me Home Now
Book Two

Chapter One

After thirty-six years of life, seducing women was second nature to Adam. In his mind, pursuing Tish was a minuscule task compared to his extensive list of conquests. Adam had watched her hips swaying rhythmically on her petite frame as she walked down the same narrow Boston Street she had gone by daily for five years on her way to work at a department store. Her job was the only thing that kept her going since her divorce from Leo, her former childhood sweetheart.

Adam parked his car beside a restaurant when he sighted her. It had been pouring rain the night before, almost like a movie set. Everything the rain had touched sparkled, and a delicious earthy scent filled the air. He almost stumbled as he rushed to get closer to her.

"Can I have a moment of your time…Do you know how I can get to…," he said, tapping Tish lightly on the shoulder from behind.

Tish turned briskly, cringing in disgust at what she considered an invasion of her personal space. As her gaze moved past Adam's broad shoulders through her medicated sunshades and landed on his face, her heart pounded furiously in her chest.

"Oh!" she exclaimed. "Do I know you?"

"I don't think so," he said, drawing his words. "I…I needed to ask you for directions. Can you spare me a couple of minutes? I promise I won't take more than that."

Tish was intuitive enough to recognize when someone needed assistance, and this wasn't the case. Adam's rugged handsome looks and mannerisms, which stood out, despite his failed attempt at stammering, screamed someone sure of himself.

"Can you offer me a little help?" Adam continued, rousing Tish from her reverie.

"Of course," Tish responded. The overpowering scent of his musky perfume filled her nostrils as he held out his hand. "Sorry. Where did you say you were going?" She was irritated by his forwardness. Rather than give her hand in return, she stepped back to create more space between them as his six-foot-two frame threatened her five feet and two inches of woman.

"Tish?" he inquired, raising his brows.

"Who told you my name?" Tish asked, looking around and then returning her gaze to him.

Adam chuckled. "Easy," he said, pointing at her jacket.

"Oh! My name tag," Tish said, heaving a sigh of relief. She had attached the tag to her jacket before leaving home that morning, a rare move for her since she often waited to settle at her stall before putting it on display. She now regretted that decision. Not only did Adam know her name without her volunteering it, but he also knew where she worked.

"It's a pretty name," Adam said, his mouth twisted in amusement.

"Still need help?" Tish said, ignoring his compliment. "Make up your mind. I'll be late for work if I don't leave now."

"I can drop you off if you—"

"No!" she responded abruptly, shaking her head. "As you already know, I'm going across the road, so I don't need a ride. Thanks for offering, though."

"Well, can I visit you sometime? I'm Adam," he said, slowly stretching out his hand, expecting her to reject it a second time.

Tish smiled from the corner of her lips as she took her right hand out of her jacket pocket and shook his. "Nice meeting you."

As she waited for him to let go of her, she began to feel a familiar stirring in her heart, one she had not experienced since the demise of her relationship with Leo. She reminded herself of her decision to avoid romantic relationships, especially not after the hand love had dealt her.

"Has anyone ever mentioned you've got gorgeous eyes?" Adam asked, looking down at her. "I imagine you receive a lot of compliments about these curly red locks of yours."

"Stop the flattery," Tish muttered. "It'll get you nowhere."

"I'm not trying to flatter you," Adam responded. "Why would you jump to that conclusion? What are you doing tonight?"

"Shouldn't you be on your way?" Tish replied with a chuckle. "On a serious note, I thought you were headed somewhere. You know you're not kidding anyone with that story. I could smell you from a mile away. I knew you didn't need any help. New Yorkers always seem to know their way around."

"You've got me! But wait, how did you know I was from New York?" Adam asked, following the direction of her gaze. "Oh! My license plate…" he said, chuckling from the realization that she'd beat him to his own game.

"You're not the only one who's observant," Tish grinned. "Hey! I have to go now. It was nice meeting you."

"Same here," he responded. "Call me when you're done with work. I'm in Boston for a few days. Perhaps we could get dinner and stop at one of the local bars for a drink. Whatever you want."

"I have dinner plans with my friends tonight."

"Ditch your friends and hang out with me," Adam pleaded.

As he handed Tish his card, her index finger brushed lightly against his, causing shockwaves down her spine. She quickly withdrew her hand and exhaled slowly to mask her racing heart.

"Maybe some other time," she said, clearing her throat and pushing a handful of hair from her face before turning to leave.

Chapter Two

Tish knew she had remained in her marriage to Leo for far too long and had worn out the patience of everyone around her. If her brother, Damascus had not rescued her that bizarre night, she would have stayed even longer. Leo had been incensed after returning from a business trip and stumbled upon a soiree Tish had organized for a small group of friends in the garden of their eight-bedroom mansion. He had waited for everyone to leave before confronting her. As an argument ensued, he dragged her around the house and bruised and battered her before disappearing into the night. She had managed to reach the phone to call Damascus to rescue her. He walked in and found her crying on the bathroom floor, and he swore to destroy her and Leo if she ever dared return to him. Damascus had alerted the police and coerced Tish to press charges. The half a dozen pictures in Damascus's possession from prior incidents helped convict Leo, otherwise, he would have gone scot-free. He now had to spend the next seven years of his life in a penitentiary.

That first encounter with Adam had left Tish disoriented, but having sworn against men, she felt too powerless to pursue things further. Her divorce was final, but she still felt the need to allow the passage of time to heal the damage caused by that relationship. Adam, on the other hand, was completely enamored of Tish. Being a lover of challenge, he became even more determined to unravel the mystery of her existence.

Following their first encounter, he frequented Boston from New York, and each time, he would visit her at work. After three attempts to get a date with her failed, he was left wondering if he had lost his charm and ability to seduce women to do his will. He had decided to ignore her for a while to give himself time to come up with a fool-proof plan to get and keep her attention. That tactic had worked exceptionally for him in the past. Some of his prior girlfriends had also played hard to get, which had made him all the more interested in them. The problem with that method was that when he finally conquered, he'd lost interest as fast as he had fallen for them, but he believed Tish was a different breed. Besides her striking good looks, there seemed to be something about her that Adam couldn't lay his hands on. The mystery of her existence, coupled with the intensity of his attraction, concerned him greatly. After six months, he had begun to feel like a loser when she continued to reject his advances. He had entered the contest on a whim.

Adam had come across the Tidal Tours website, the host of the "Love Experiment." When he googled "how to get the love you want." The even-numbered contestants in this experiment provided information about their situation as well as details regarding the targeted odd-numbered contestant they desired to fall in love with. They then waited to see if their object of desire would take the bait through a carefully planned strategy to woo them into entering the competition by positioning their agents in strategic locations that their targets frequented in a bid to lure them to enter the contest.

Tish was Contestant 103, and Adam, being 104, was completely in cahoots with the organizers. "Three months in the tropics, by the beach, with nothing to do, will surely make someone fall in love with you," the website promised. The rules of the game prohibited the contestants from revealing their true identities. They were expected to play along as they were automatically matched with the object of their desire. The contest was rigged to favor the even-numbered contestants, labeled evens, as they enticed the odd-numbered contestants, labeled odds, who were led to believe they were playing a fair game. The evens received different contest rules than the odds. For them, swiping left and right on the Q phone was a mere formality. Their target was already set. To retain their advantage, the evens were to play exactly as instructed to get that love they wanted. The hosts supplied them with lines to help them pull in their odd-numbered conquest and coerce them to declare their love for one another by the time both parties returned their Q phones.

Tish's entanglement with Leo was not the only thing weighing her down as she walked home the day she received the news that she had won the contest. The office politics instigated by Abhiri, the unofficial office gossip, made her life unbearable. She knew exactly how the report that she was gunning for the supervisor's job started. Her words had been misconstrued during a conversation she had with Abhiri earlier that week. Following that conversation, she had felt uneasy but failed to realize how much things could be twisted out of context. In the days that followed, her supervisor had passed by her stall several times without uttering as much as a hello. She had also made an unreasonable number of requests of Tish. Abhiri had joined the team only a year prior and desperately sought Tish's friendship when she noticed none of the old-timers would give her the time of day. Tish now blamed herself for letting her guard down and allowing Abhiri into her circle, a trait that did not come so naturally to her.

Tish's heart raced when she saw a blue envelope sticking out of the mailbox attached to her front wall as she arrived at her doorstep. It looked nothing like the regular pieces of junk mail she had grown accustomed to receiving from the department stores in the area. She winced at the clanging sound as she pulled the envelope out of the old rusty mailbox. This one was addressed specifically to her and bore no postmark.

"They just brought that," her next-door neighbor Pat said in a voice loud enough for anyone within a mile to hear.

"Who?" Tish asked.

"Two blokes in a Tidal Tours SUV."

"Did you say Tidal Tours?"

"Yep! They asked for you and I told them you'd be back soon. Always back at the same time. A creature of habit you are, Miss Tish! How was your day?"

"It was…It is now wonderful…Sort of," Tish muttered.

"Do have a good evening, dear. Let me know if you'll like some of that soup."

"I definitely will," Tish said, rushing to her basement apartment, almost tripping at the entrance. She headed straight for the living room, where she set down her tote at the center table before tearing open the envelope to reveal what was inside. Her legs weakened, and her heart almost jumped out of her mouth when she realized she had been selected as a winner in the Dream Voyage contest. She pushed the week-old laundry lying on the couch onto the floor and crashed into it before grabbing her phone to dial the phone number on the card she pulled out of the envelope.

"Congratulations on your win," A male voice with a musical monotone answered after a few rings. "You must be very happy to have been selected for our grand prize in the contest."

"Are you for real?" Tish asked, jumping on her feet to quench her sudden desire to scream at the top of her lungs.

"If you mean Tidal Tours…Yes, as real as you'd like us to be."

"Wait…How did you know I was the one calling?" Tish asked, trying her best to hide her excitement.

"Our record keeping here at Tidal Tours is quite meticulous. Your phone number is in our database. Does that answer your question?"

"I think so," she muttered.

"We'd like you to come to our office to sign some contracts," the man said. "Will you be able to make it before the end of the day? We'd like to get this out of the way as soon as possible so you can begin to enjoy your prize."

"I'm a bit tired from work but I can make it before the end of the day," Tish replied after pausing for a moment. "Please excuse me. I'm still in awe. I never knew this was remotely possible. I entered the contest just for the sake of it. The old man was quite persuasive."

"Well then, I just sent an address to your email. Bring three pieces of ID. We'll see you soon," the voice on the other end said and hung up.

There was no doubt in Tish's mind about what her next course of action was. Providence had instructed her to pay attention to the elderly gentleman waving a flier in her direction as she stopped for a snack at the convenience store near her apartment. Her first instinct was to keep going, but as the gentleman insisted she take one, a voice inside her head convinced her to stop. She had forgotten the encounter for weeks until the flier fell out of her wallet as she pulled out her credit card to pay for groceries. The grand prize, an all-expense-paid trip to Costa Rica for a period agreed upon by the contest promoters and the winners, was too tempting to ignore. That very day, she entered the contest online. Though she had sworn off love after her experience with Leo and was only interested in the adventure, the catch—that contestants would receive a brand-new Q phone with an advanced dating app configured to help them find their one true love, had not deterred her.

She received her Q phone the following day, and with each swipe, she began to relinquish her cynicism and started to make connections. 104 was the ultimate connection for her. Since the rules prohibited the contestants from revealing their true identities to each other, she relied on the ranking of his physical characteristics on a rating scale to determine what he looked like. During the two-month dating period, the emotions ignited through her interactions with 104 helped her to let go of her inhibitions and Leo. Her heart awakened as she looked forward to 104's messages and found herself texting him about all aspects of her day. She was developing a seamless connection without realizing it, creeping onto her as though she had known 104 all her life. When the contest was winding down and the time came to submit her phone at the specified drop box location, she fell into deep sadness. Since the contestants were not allowed contact until notified, she remained on edge and waited for the organizers to announce the winners, but she never imagined in a million years that she would be chosen as a winner.

Chapter Three

The contract signing was straightforward. She would usually pay attention to the fine print or even ask her lawyer friend to review it, but this time, a quick look told her it was the same legal stuff she had grown accustomed to. To her, it was less complicated than what she had to deal with when she purchased her apartment or even the piles of information she had to get through during her messy divorce. She could not imagine what could go wrong in the current circumstances. Time was of the essence, and she felt she understood enough not to expend her energy poring over the meaning behind the words on the sheets of paper presented to her by Tidal Tours. If the past five years had taught her anything, it would be that nothing in life is guaranteed, and this may well be her chance at happiness.

"I am so happy for you!" Tish's mother said after she called to give her the good news. "Have you told Damascus?"

"Not yet. I just got home from their office."

"So when do you leave?

"Tomorrow morning," Tish replied while going over the outfits she had carefully laid out on the bed.

"So soon? Does that mean I won't even see you for Sunday brunch?" her mother said despairingly.

"I wish I could have stayed till then," Tish interjected. "But it's not every day you get the opportunity to visit Costa Rica and leave all your troubles behind. There's nothing here for me...I mean absolutely nothing!"

"Don't say that," her mother cautioned. "You have a great job and you have me and your brother."

"I don't mean you guys," Tish said defensively. "It's everything else. I'm happy to be going somewhere Leo could never think of reaching me. I'm so tired of his shenanigans. The prank calls I've been receiving lately spouting the importance of forgiveness have his name written all over it. He keeps trying to contact me despite the court-imposed no-contact provision. He'll be out in a year and I want to be in a completely different place when that happens. I know he's going to come running to me as soon as the protection order runs out. I'll consider myself pathetic if I were to give him the time of day."

"There's nothing pathetic about you. Not as far as I'm concerned. He's the one who made the mistakes. Renew the protection order if you need to, and if he dares bother you, we'll make it permanent. You're a beautiful girl. You have no reason to feel ashamed."

"I hear you, Mom. I wish I had as much faith in myself as you do."

"You have to take it one day at a time," her mother responded shakily. "It will come. Just be patient."

"Ok. I need to go now. Lots of packing to do," Tish said, cracking under the strain of the emotions that suddenly coursed through her. It was inevitable, but she hated these reminders that her life so far left much to be desired. As her mother suggested, she was doing what she could to turn it around. The contest, her conquest, the trip she was about to embark on, all of it, was evidence she was doing something to fix things.

"Don't forget to tell Damascus," Her mother continued, interrupting her thoughts.

"No problem," Tish responded. "And I'll try to call you every day. Take good care of yourself."

"You too. Have fun."

Tish kept her promise and called Damascus as soon as her mother hung up.

"That's such a long time for you to be away," he said after Tish told him everything. "Will I be able to visit?"

"I don't think so," she responded with a chuckle. "I'll call you whenever I get the chance. I told Mom the same thing."

Tish was glad visitors were not an option. Her dream was to head anywhere other than where she was, and that included escaping from everyone and everything she knew. She loved her brother, and he had done so much for her, but not even he could make her feel guilty for taking this time for herself.

"We'll all be waiting for that call," Damascus finally said. "Sad to see you leave, but happy for you, little sis."

"Thank you, Damascus."

Tish barely slept that night as her mind went around in circles, wondering what the future would bring. She tossed and turned in bed, unable to bring herself to close her eyes, her mind consumed by thoughts of the unknown. She knew that whatever was coming would be a major turning point, and she couldn't help but feel both excited and terrified at the same time. Her life was about to begin all over. *Could that happen?* She wondered. For someone who was a realist and didn't have stock in the tooth fairy, she desperately hoped she could have a do-over.

Chapter Four

Tish left for Costa Rica the following day aboard a Costa Airlines flight. Right after she spoke to her brother the night before, she called her boss to ask for an emergency leave of absence for the next three months. She had outrightly denied the request and made clear that if Tish decided to carry on with her plans, she might as well say a big farewell to her job. Tish happily agreed to say farewell. There was no point for her to remain in a toxic environment when she could be cruising around the world. The ultimatum gave her an excuse to extend her stay beyond three months.

Ty from Tidal Tours welcomed her at the airport after customs clearance. He whisked her to baggage claims, where he helped take her luggage out of the carousel before ushering her into the black limousine waiting at the entrance.

"Welcome to Costa Rica," he said, joining the driver in the front seat. "I'm Ty."

"Thank you so much. And I'm Tish. How long is the ride to my hotel?"

"Close to an hour. Really depends on traffic," Ty said, placing his elbows on the window.

"Hmm. That'll give me the chance to catch some sleep."

Having not slept the night before, Tish's mind and body rebelled from exhaustion. Her eyelids came down like the shutters in Moulin Rouge after she laid her head on the back seat. She snoozed the entire ride from the airport, only waking when Ty announced they had arrived at the lodgings. The orange sun had taken over the horizon but was slowly disappearing behind the glistening blue waters. Her yawn overtook her while she took in the view of miles of white sand, swaying coconut trees, and beautiful vegetation. The limousine pulled to the front of the twenty-four-story luxury apartment complex with its beautiful fountains, swimming pool, and tennis court in the far corner.

She was taken aback by the warm, dense air that hit her face the moment she stepped out of the limousine. The smell of salt water, mixed with smoke from the barbecues cooking in different parts of the complex, tickled her senses. The building was bustling with vacationers in various states of undress. The longer she stared at them, the more her feelings erupted as she daydreamed about her rendezvous with 104.

"When will I meet Contestant 104?" she asked

"He's arriving tomorrow," Ty responded matter-of-factly.

"What's one more night?" Tish responded, suddenly enveloped by shyness.

As they passed the lobby on their way to the elevator, she scanned the faces of the men and women in her path and wondered if any of them belonged to any of the other contestants.

"Are the other contestants living in this building?" she asked Ty after he stepped aside for her to enter the elevator before him.

"I'm not privy to that information," he responded. "I know you're scheduled to meet 104 and that's it. Sorry, I couldn't be of more help."

"That's okay. It's just that I could swear that earlier, you said you could answer all my questions."

"Hey…If you have questions regarding your schedule or 104's, I'll be able to address them. I'm not allowed to…Or let me put it this way…For privacy reasons, I'm not permitted to share information about the others with you."

"I understand," Tish muttered, slightly embarrassed. The initial excitement she felt when she arrived slowly turned to nerves. She felt like a high school girl about to go on her first date, and that was something she never wanted to experience again.

"Let me know if you need anything else," Ty continued as they stopped outside her door. "Here's my number," he concluded, handing Tish a business card with a number typed in bold letters before walking toward the direction of the elevator.

Tish sang a tune while she bathed and reminisced about the events of the past few years, at intervals, heaving a huge sigh of relief that she finally got the chance to escape. She knew not many could boast of such an opportunity. As her thoughts drifted to her first date with Leo, what he wore, and how he made her feel, she quickly cautioned herself to snap back to the present and leave the past where it belonged.

After she came out of the tub, she tied a towel around her chest and started taking her clothes out of her luggage and placing them on the bed. Just as she was about to hang them in the closet, which was hidden behind a large wooden door, she heard a beeping sound that stopped soon after it started. The sound was barely audible, but it was loud enough for her to know with certainty that it had come from the four corners of the small studio apartment. Unsure of what to make of it, she paused and darted her eyes around the room to see if a light would give away the source, perking her ears and waiting for a repeat so she could take action. When she heard nothing, she continued hanging her clothes and dancing to the tune playing in her head.

Dinner was waiting on the writing desk and had been there since she arrived. The smell of the meal filled the room and made her stomach growl in anticipation. She couldn't help but feel grateful for the thoughtful gesture. However, the large meal left her feeling heavy and bloated. She decided to throw on a short slip dress and take a walk around the complex to try and walk off the discomfort. Besides the bloating, her mind was consumed with thoughts of meeting 104 in the morning. She knew she needed to clear her head and relax in order to fully enjoy her vacation.

Calypso music blasted in the distance as she stepped out of the elevator. Outside, a full moon drifted in the sky. She sighted the limousine that had dropped her off earlier. Looking closer, she realized Ty was sitting in the front seat, and a shiver ran through her spine as she recalled his evasiveness when she questioned him about the others. After he stepped out, he opened the back door for a man and a woman, and they exchanged a few words before the limousine drove off with him in the back seat. The couple seemed to be engaged in a heated argument as they walked into the lobby, with each side making extreme effort to get their point across.

Tish grimaced and studied the couple closely as they approached. The man was well-toned, and by the way he angled his head while he spoke to the woman, Tish could tell he was angry. The woman was of slim build, had silky dark hair, and an obvious pout on her lips. Tish held her breath as she overheard the man addressing the woman in a tone that was not particularly gentlemanly.

"Jesse, if you would have simply told me what you were up to, we wouldn't be in this shit," he said.

"What do you mean, Eli? Would you have preferred to remain in our dingy townhouse in Boston right now? If I recall, you were running as fast as you could to get away from me and come here. You didn't even tell me where you were going until mere hours before you were supposed to leave. I had to drag every piece of information out of you. Your actions left me no choice." Jesse spoke with intense anguish in her tone.

"Tell me one more time, Jesse," Eli continued, glaring at her. "What was I running from? And, how has my lot improved? How?"

Tish had become entranced as she listened to them and failed to look where she was going, nearly bumping into Eli.

"Excuse me," Eli said, eyeing her angrily.

"I'm sorry," Tish said, retreating slowly.

"Watch where you're going next time," he cautioned.

Before Tish could respond, they resumed their argument as they headed for the elevator, but their voices soon faded into the distance. Tish wished she could be a fly on the wall at that moment as that would have allowed her access to more of their intriguing conversation. Had she mastered the art of discretion and not bumped into

Eli earlier, she may have been granted an elevator ride with this fascinating pair and perhaps an introduction. She did not know them, but for some reason, she felt they had information that may be of interest to her. For one, they were from Boston, and they knew Ty. When she first sighted them with Ty, she'd imagined they could be matches in the "Dream Voyage" contest, but with the manner they spoke as if they'd known each other for ages, she decided she could be mistaken. The more she thought about them, the more she became concerned about the "situation" they had been referring to. Soon, a lightbulb flashed through her head, and she threw caution to the wind and ran in the direction of the elevator to confront the woman.

"Hold it!" she pleaded. She was so close she could almost touch the door with her fingertips.

Eli raised his brows while Jesse waved an apologetic hand as the door shut right in front of her.

It seemed to Tish they had intentionally disregarded her request, but she brushed it off and convinced herself she had given it her best shot and decided to continue on her mission. She headed out of the lobby and followed the sound of music. The smell of ram barbecue teased her nostrils while she roamed amongst the crowd at the outdoor party in the far north section of the complex. The variety of odors soon overpowered the smell of the barbecue, and the longer she stayed, the more she lost control of her senses, causing her to succumb to the wiles of the twenty-something-year-old man who kept pushing her to have yet another drink. A little past midnight and six drinks later, a chilly wind began to blow, her cue to go to bed to receive 104 when he arrived the next day.

Chapter Five

His cheeky smile and angular jaw were what she noticed first when she opened the door before sunset the next day, but it couldn't be. A second later, those pale blue eyes looked down at her with half trepidation and half excitement. All that, coupled with the musky smell of the same scent he wore when they first met on that narrow Boston Street, caused her head to swoon. He caught her as she almost stumbled on the marble floor.

"Adam?"

"Yes?"

"What…What are you doing here? Aren't you supposed to be in New York?"

He chuckled as she slowly pried herself away from his arms and adjusted her shirt, which had slipped off her shoulders and was beginning to show a bit of cleavage by the time she recovered her senses.

"Tish, I'm 104."

Tish's cheeks paled, her eyes widening in shock as she watched Adam. The words he just said were like daggers, stabbing into her heart.

"You're 104? Adam, you're lying to me," she squealed, shaking her head as she slowly edged back towards the queen-sized bed positioned precisely in the center of the room before sinking into it. "What is going on? Can you tell the truth about what you're really doing here?" She continued to stare at him, struggling to make sense of the image of the man standing before her.

"I already told you all there is to tell. I'm not sure what type of explanation you need," he said with a wide grin. "Would you like me to leave? For some reason, I thought you'd be happy to find out it was me. Guess I was wrong."

"Adam," Tish continued. Her voice was softer this time, the edges of defiance replaced by a subtle vulnerability. "You still haven't told me anything that can help me make sense of this situation."

As she waited for an answer from Adam, she recalled her encounter with Eli and Jesse from the night before. "Oh!" was all she could mutter as she continued to gaze at Adam's towering frame, unsure about what to do with him. If he really was 104, then it would be wrong of her to accept his offer to leave. He couldn't possibly be stalking her all the way from Boston. She didn't think he had it in him and judging from her experience the night before, it could very well be that Adam was who he said he was. She took one more look at him. He had one hand in his pocket, and with the other hand, he was holding onto the handle of his briefcase patiently waiting for her to come out of her head.

"Has it sunk in now?" Adam said with a nervous chuckle. "I am so sorry that I freaked you out when I first walked in. I'll do my best to clear things up."

"Go on. I'm listening," Tish said.

"I'm 104. The same person you've been communicating with. The man you fell in love with."

"Is this a conspiracy?" Tish asked when he paused to wait for what he said to sink in. She was doing the best she could to hide her annoyance.

"There's no conspiracy, at least not one to harm you, Tish," Adam said. "I can see you're not excited to see me. You're not thrilled with this whole thing. Although it hurts my feelings, I don't blame you one bit. I know it may be too much to ask, but I'd like to know how you feel. Are you okay? You don't look so good right now!"

"Would you feel good if you were in my shoes?" Tish retorted eyeing him surreptitiously.

"I get it. You need time…I'll clue you in once I get off these clothes. Where is the bathroom? I promise I'll tell you everything, but you'll have to give me the chance to explain."

"I'm looking forward to that. There," Tish said, pointing in the direction of the bathroom.

The Love Experiment rules had prohibited the even-numbered contestants from revealing the intricacies of the game during the contest, but nothing stopped them from sharing the details of the experiment and their reason for involving their conquest after the fact — after they had reunited with the odd-numbered contestant in Costa Rica. Tish was never one to sit idly by and wait for things to happen. This was a quality that both served her well and got her into trouble when she least expected it. As soon as Adam emerged from the bathroom looking handsome in an all-white ensemble — a fitted linen shirt, pants, and leather sandals, she went straight to the point. "What is it you've still not told me, Adam?"

"Won't you at least first let me know what side of the bed is mine? Or will I be relegated to the couch?" Adam asked with a nervous smile.

"Please answer me," Tish pleaded, adjusting herself on the bed and tossing her head backwards. "This is no time for jokes."

Adam had forgotten how stunning she was as she stared at him with beautiful green eyes that changed hue the longer he looked at them. Her lavender scent hit his nostrils as he moved closer and leaned forward to kiss her cheeks. She allowed him but withdrew the second he tried to hold her hand and pointed to the chair in the corner. She needed to create some distance between them to avoid blurring the boundaries before she had the chance to get answers to what was at the top of her mind.

Adam sat down on the edge of the chair and confessed everything to Tish. When he finished, he stood up and walked towards the window, turning his back to her.

"I hope you're not upset," he said after an uncomfortable silence followed.

"You hope I'm not upset? That's a ridiculous statement," Tish responded with a light-hearted laugh.

Tish had lived most of her life as one that was described by most as prim and proper. There was no way signing up for this adventure, her attempt to shake off that reputation and live a more exciting life could be upsetting to her. She welcomed the challenge. Prim and proper had gotten her nowhere. It had led her to the violent life she shared with Leo. Nothing could be more upsetting than that. Although the words she said to Adam had portrayed sarcasm, her countenance had changed to that of a person who was unbothered.

"So what then? Are you furious?" Adam asked, breaking the wall of silence that had built between them.

"Surprisingly not," Tish chirped after hesitating for a second. I'm flattered that you went to such heights to go out with me. I had sworn to never love again after my experience with Leo but, I decided to keep an open mind during this experiment. The only problem I have now is that I'm not sure if everything I've experienced so far with you is real."

"It was all real!" Adam blurted, immediately turning on his heel, backing away from the window, and heading towards Tish." The mixed messages Tish's body language was giving off scared Adam more than anything. It gave him more cause for concern than her initial reaction when he came in. Bad as that was, he had somehow expected that. This new Tish presented a different challenge, one he was not sure his usual charm was prepared to handle. "It was as real as anything can be," Adam insisted, holding onto the hope that he'd be able to convince her to see his point of view.

Tish chuckled nervously and shook her head. "I don't know what to believe anymore. You tricked me. You knew it was me the whole time. Whereas, I, on my part was going through what I thought was a genuine love experiment."

"Don't say that," Adam responded, flailing his hands in every direction.

"Why not?" Tish insisted. "I refused your advances in reality for good reason."

"Because of Leo?"

Tish stared at Adam in frustration, her eyes narrowing as she tried to suppress the rising tide of irritation within her. "It's so wrong for you to mention that," she muttered angrily. "You know so much about my personal life from our dating experience but that does not give you the right to bring Leo up so casually. I shared those things in confidence. Why throw it in my face?"

"I'm sorry," Adam said, edging closer to her. "you mentioned him earlier, so I thought it was okay."

"It's not okay but let's move on. I had my reasons for not dating you in reality," Tish continued. "It had nothing to do with my ex. It had everything to do with you," she said, gesticulating wildly.

"Something to do with me?" Adam said wide-eyed.

"Why are you acting so surprised? I heard that after I refused your advances, you started sleeping with Samira in my office."

"What?" Adam balked. "I never slept with Samira."

"I wasn't mad," Tish continued. "Hey, you're free to date or sleep with whomever you want. I just couldn't take you seriously after that."

"Tish, listen to me," Adam said, staring into her eyes. "You're the only woman I want. Samira and I are just friends. I didn't sleep with her. Was that why you kept on rejecting me? Because of Samira?" He finished with a nervous laugh.

Tish turned to look at him. "Okay, but how do I know you're not playing games now?"

"Why would I go through all this to get to you if my intention was to play games?" he said sincerely.

"I don't know," Tish said, looking away. "Why do humans act irrationally?"

"Are you referring to me?" he responded, his brows knitted.

"I don't know. I'm still trying to process all of this."

Adam came closer and sat beside Tish on the bed. When he brushed his arm lightly against hers, he could feel his heart racing as he had no idea what to say next, or even how to act. But when Tish turned, and he saw a hint of a smile form on her lips, he began to loosen up. At that moment, he knew that he had been given a second chance. A chance to make things right, to start anew. "Hey, let's go somewhere and chill," he said, nudging Tish on her side. "We can continue our discussion on the way."

Tish offered a sympathetic smile. "Not a bad idea. Where are you taking—"

The sound of a beep caught Adam's attention and he quickly stood up from the bed, looking around in surprise. He glanced in every corner of the room, his eyes widening as he tried to figure out the source of the sound. "What is that weird sound?" he asked.

"I forgot to ask you about that!" Tish exclaimed, grabbing Adam's hand and pulling him back on the bed. "Was this part of the deal?"

"What do you mean? I thought the sound was coming from your phone," Adam said.

"Nope," Tish responded, shaking her head. "Did that sound like a phone to you? This is the second time I've heard that sound since I arrived. It's freaky. Isn't it?"

"It is, but I don't think we need to panic," Adam said, grabbing Tish's hand to help her up from the bed. "Maybe it's the central air conditioning. Something may need servicing."

"I hope so," Tish said. "I imagined much worse. I was worried there could be some voyeuristic activity going on here. You know, recording intimate moments."

"Why would anyone do that in a place like this?" Adam asked.

"I don't know!" Tish exclaimed. "Why would anyone do anything they're not supposed to do? For the kicks."

"Try to be more trusting."

Tish was not one to trust people or things at face value. Yet, after finding out Adam and the organizers had led her on, she allowed Adam to remain by her side. She knew what she felt during the dating process with her Q phone. It felt like love. It could have been love. She had trusted him as much as she could and was willing to lean in a little more if it meant getting the second chance she sincerely craved. *What was she to do now when 104 was in on it? How could she trust anything he told her?* The fact that 104 was in on the deception made things even more complicated. Tish now had to question every word that came out of Adam's mouth, wondering if he was being honest or if he was just playing another game. It was difficult for her to know what to believe and who to trust.

Despite her doubts, Tish still held onto the hope that she could salvage something from this situation. She desperately wanted a second chance and was willing to give Adam the benefit of the doubt, even though he had been a part of the deception.

"Tish?" Adam called, jolting her out of reverie.

"I hear you, Adam," she said. "I'm not taking any more chances. On our way out, I'll carry the few valuables I brought with me, just in case."

"That should not be a problem."

Chapter Six

Adam had planned an elaborate outing for the two of them. After a long conversation trying to find out everything they could about the other person, while munching on a plate of fish and chips, they danced to calypso music at a nightclub by the beach.

Tish could feel Adam's body pressing against hers, sending waves of pleasure through her entire frame. His hand roamed over her back, and she felt herself getting lost in the moment, completely consumed by passion.

"I hope you're having a good time," Adam whispered as his lips lingered languorously on hers.

Unable to resist him, Tish let go of all her inhibitions and kissed him back until her knees started to buckle. The heat between them was so intense that any onlooker would have assumed that they had been waiting for this moment for an eternity. Their lips moved in perfect harmony, each kiss deeper and more desperate than the last. She could feel the desire coursing through her veins as his hands continued to explore her body, igniting a fire within her.

Tish didn't want the moment to end, but eventually, they had to come up for air. As they broke the kiss, she looked into his eyes, seeing the same desire and longing reflected in them.

"We shouldn't be doing this," Tish said breathlessly, her lips still exploring his mouth.

"Why?" he whispered.

"Because…Because…It's too soon."

"Says who?" Adam mumbled and swiftly pulled her closer, causing her to gasp.

As her body trembled and melted in his arms, he slid his hands down her back and caressed it slowly in an up-and-down motion as he swayed from side to side. Tish felt as though she was drowning in her own emotions with no willpower left to stop him. Then again, she didn't see the need to. In her mind, he was a perfect gentleman on that date, their very first since meeting several months back.

They danced for a few more minutes until the dance floor became too crowded and smoky. Settling in a corner, they sipped some *guaro* until Tish's head started to spin.

"You look tipsy," Adam yelled over the loud music.

"Yeah. A little bit," Tish giggled.

"Should we call it a day?"

"I think so," she said.

Adam immediately stepped down from his stool and helped her dismount.

"Thank you," she whispered. "I had such a good time."

"We should do it again tomorrow."

"Sure. We should."

After they left the club, they walked around the apartment complex silently, holding hands. Tish began to worry about her behavior at the club. She wondered if she had given up too much too soon with the way she kissed Adam on the dance floor. As the silence persisted, she let her mind wander to other things, including the mysterious couple she met the night before. She perused the faces of the passersby, hoping to see Eli and Jesse again.

"You seem preoccupied with something," Adam stated. "Are you still bothered about the sound in the room? Trust me, it's nothing!"

"I'm not sure that it's nothing," she said, shaking her head. "Anyway, I was actually thinking about something else. I felt worse about the sound in the room after I eavesdropped on a private conversation last night. That encounter put me on edge."

"You know what they say about eavesdroppers?" Adam joked.

"Stop kidding," Tish laughed. "There was something about how that couple was acting that made me think there was more to the sound. I still can't shake the feeling."

"Did they look like swingers?"

"Oh, nothing like that," Tish said, shaking her head. "I ran into them when I was heading out to get some fresh air. I think their names are Eli and Jesse. Ty, the same guy that picked me up from the airport had dropped them off in the same limo that he picked me up in. When I heard them talking about something that was obviously getting both of them so riled up, that they were almost coming to blows, I began to imagine there was so much more to this whole thing. I tried to follow them but they…the guy was too pissed to let me in the elevator with them. I know it feels like I've asked you this a million times, but I'll ask you one more time. Is there something you haven't told me?"

"About what exactly?"

"This whole experience," Tish said exasperatedly.

"No," Adam responded stopping to place both hands firmly on her shoulders. "As far as I know, this is an experiment to find one's true love. Don't you feel anything for me at all?" he asked staring into her eyes for answers.

Tish looked away, chuckling.

"Do you feel anything?" Adam repeated in a serious tone.

"I don't know…I can't say how I feel with certainty. There may be something there, but I don't know," Tish answered with a sigh. "It may take some time, though."

"Then there's nothing more to tell."

They headed back to their room long past midnight, choosing to bypass the elevators and take the long flight of stairs, giggling as they went along. When they finally arrived at the fifth floor, where their room was located, they were content and exhausted from their adventure.

"I knew it!" Tish exclaimed, gasping as they stood outside their door.

"What, Tish?" Adam said calmly.

"Okay, I didn't reveal this to you, but before we left, I placed a thin strip of paper there," she said, pointing at the top of the door. "I secured it with transparent tape. It's a trick I learned way back in the day when I was a Girl Scout. Look, the strip is broken, and this can only mean one thing — someone entered this room when we were out."

"Could it have just fallen off?" Adam said casually.

"No, no," Tish said, shaking her head furiously. "That's the point of the tape. It was secured."

"Honestly Tish. I don't know what to say. This little setup is brilliant, but I wonder what anyone will want with our stuff in this high-end apartment complex. I've seen some of the patrons, they all look so dignified. Could this have been a mistake?"

Tish stared at Adam wide-eyed. "Mistake?" she groaned. "Someone entered our room without our consent and they could still be in there right now. How could you be so unperturbed? I'm not going in there. Call security."

"Come," Adam said, holding her hand and walking in. "See, there is no one here," he continued, speaking at the top of his voice to alert any possible intruder and keep Tish at ease.

"I'm still not okay with this. I know I said I wouldn't do this, not after how fast he disappeared after showing me the place, but I'll have to call Ty. This isn't what I signed up for."

"What are you going to tell him?"

"That I've had enough."

"Really? We haven't even started. Are you going to quit before you give this a chance?" Adam said, pointing back and forth.

"I meant what I said. I'm calling him now," Tish said, dialing Ty's number on her cell phone, later giving up after Ty did not pick up after several rings.

"He's probably asleep by now," Adam said after he saw the worried look on Tish's face. We'll call him again tomorrow. I'm sure there's a perfectly good explanation for this. Let's settle down and have some wine to relax a bit."

"Give me a moment to process this," she said collapsing on a chair.

Just as Adam was about to plead with her to remain calm and think logically, the beep sounded again.

On hearing that, Tish sprang up from the chair and threw her hands in the air. "There is no way I'm sleeping here! Pack your things," she said, breathing heavily as she paced back and forth in the living room.

"Where would we go, Tish?"

"Anywhere but here," she said, gathering her belongings. "Adam, you're not moving," she yelled when she noticed he was standing in one place, aghast. "How can we stay here after everything that's just happened? We can find somewhere to stay tonight, and then tomorrow, we can try to contact the organizers since Ty is not picking up his calls."

"Do you know anyone in Guanacaste?" Adam asked when he finally mustered the strength to speak.

"No. But what does that have to do with anything? We could always book a hotel."

Right after she uttered those words, Tish knew what she was proposing was not plausible at that time of the night, especially so far away from home. And she didn't need much convincing after Adam placed both hands on her shoulder to calm her. "Let's go to sleep instead," he pleaded. "We'll resolve this in the morning."

Chapter Seven

Tish woke up feeling as though she had been pulled by a truck for miles with a ton of bricks attached to her head. A sickly smell, a cross between the odor of rusty metal and vinegar, wafted around her. She was facing upwards, her least favorite sleeping position, as she always woke up with strange nightmares whenever she was not lying on her side. As much as she tried, she soon realized it was impossible to take her preferred posture as her body was frozen to the spot. When she finally remembered where she was, she opened her mouth to call Adam, but only a whisper came out. She groaned as she moved her head to the right, to the bed beside her. Like her, Adam was lying on his back, facing upwards, stiff like a log, with no sound coming from him. The harsh morning light was seeping through the curtains, and the room spun as she attempted to sit up, limbs protesting with each movement.

"Adam!" Her voice remained a whisper. "Adam!" No sound. As she struggled to piece together the fragments of her hazy memory, a faint recollection of the events from the night before emerged. The memories were like scattered puzzle pieces, and Tish tried to connect them as she surveyed the room. An empty wine bottle, crumpled chocolate wraps, and a couple of wine glasses adorned the table at the center of the room, offering subtle hints of the activities that may have taken place.

The last thing she could remember was dancing and having fun with Adam on their date. Nothing else would come to mind, so she concluded Adam had either drugged her *guaro* at the nightclub or the wine she drank after they returned to their apartment. That eerie thought stayed with her for only a minute before she returned her gaze to the ceiling and attempted to move once more. A piercing pain shot through her chest cavity, and she called Adam again, but Adam still did not respond.

When her bladder began to burst with urine, she shifted one leg at a time to the floor, crouched forward, and lifted her body slowly to head to the bathroom. Her legs could barely carry her, so she stumbled and fell next to Adam's bed and lay there crying for a few minutes until she began to feel intense aches and pains throughout her body.

"Adam, Adam," she called, shaking his leg, pausing at intervals to see if he would respond.

"What…?" he finally mumbled.

"Adam, I don't feel good," she said, leaning on his footboard, later dragging herself up and shuffling towards the bathroom when Adam did not respond further.

She removed her robe with great difficulty when she finally made it to the bathroom. The soft hum of the ventilation fan provided a soothing background noise, and Tish closed her eyes as she sat on the toilet seat, allowing herself a moment's rest. The bathroom became a sanctuary of solitude, shielding her from the harsh reality of her physical state, and calming her racing mind. But as she started to stand up to turn on the tap, a sudden dizziness washed over her.

"No!" she shrieked, steadying herself against the bathroom counter. The room seemed to spin, and Tish felt a surge of nausea. She decided to sit down on the edge of the bathtub, hoping the sensation would pass.

Just as she lowered herself, the dizziness intensified, and at that very moment, she caught a glimpse of herself in the bathroom mirror. Pale and disoriented, she barely recognized the person staring back at her. Though the view was blurry, the shock of what she could make out caused her to tremble. As her eyes moved from her messy hair to her patchy skin, she realized her body had gone through unimaginable torture, and she'd probably been asleep for longer than a day. Tears rolled down her cheeks, and as she raised her hand to wipe some of it away, she felt that piercing pain in her chest again.

A slow trickle ran from her cleavage to the fold under her breast and slowly drifted down to her navel at the same time that a pink liquid rapidly spread through her white nightshirt. She raised the shirt in panic and gasped in horror. A jagged line ran from her chest, past the center of her breasts, and ended near her ribcage. At the sight, she collapsed on the bathroom floor, hitting her head on the bathtub. The last thing she heard was the echo of her own gasp before everything went silent.

Take Me Home Now
Book Three

Chapter One

"Tish…Tiish…Tiiish…Can you hear me?" the nurse whispered, gently caressing Tish's shoulder while she muttered, "Take me home now…Take me home now," as she convulsed under the blanket. Her half-shut eyes dripped with tears. Some rolled down the side of her face, landing freely on her curly red hair, which was sprawled all over the flimsy hospital pillow.

"It's okay. You're fine now," the nurse continued, applying light pressure on Tish's shoulder, causing her to spasm and move her head from side to side as though frantic to break free from a powerful force causing her unimaginable harm.

"Where am I?" Tish asked, wide-eyed, wriggling to escape from the nurse's grip, still unable to grasp her condition as she stared at her face, looking for answers.

"You're safe. We're in the Jand clinic," the nurse assured her, slowly loosening her hold and signaling her to remain still. "I wouldn't move if I were you. You do not want to open those wounds."

"Wounds?" Tish gasped, immediately moving her right hand to her chest, where she was starting to get a tight feeling. "What…What happened to me? How did I get here?"

"Please be patient. I'll get the doctor right away. He's the one that can answer all your questions," the nurse said as she exited the room, muttering a few words in Spanish.

After she left, Tish altered her gaze from the stained ceilings to the ill-plastered walls in the ward, which seemed to move closer the longer she stared at it. In her mind, the glossy pink pastel oil paint would have been more appropriate for an indoor garden, not for a crowded hospital ward where it left a crippling feeling of hopelessness.

There were at least six other beds in the room, each with an occupant at a different level of discomfort. The patient on her left had one leg hanging in the air, and the one on the far right had tubes entering and exiting different parts of his body. Tish scanned the room and wished she could talk to each of them to hear their stories, but she knew that was not feasible in her condition. Instead, she focused on the patient to her left. The lady looked so frail, and there was something oddly familiar about her. It took her some time, but she recognized Jesse. Her long, black, silky hair hung down the side of the bed as she slept in fits and starts. Her pale white skin carried the tell-tale sign of someone who had not seen the sun for days. The most striking thing was her facial features. Not only did they seem more pronounced than the night she ran into her when she first arrived in Costa Rica, but they also looked like they belonged to someone who had conceded defeat.

Across from Jesse was Eli. He was seated upright in the bed and gave her a little wave when their eyes met. Eli's friendly gesture brought back memories of their initial meeting. It was a far cry from his behaviour the night they met. He had been seriously unfriendly, but now, as she looked into his tired eyes, she couldn't help but feel a sense of sadness. Feeling too numb to reciprocate but worried he could label her rude, she merely nodded at him. At that moment, a strong scent of antiseptic filled the room, suffocating her, therefore causing her to gag and shift her position on the bed. She sobbed loudly as the tightness in her chest turned to piercing pain.

"Are you okay?" Eli asked exasperatedly.

"No," Tish responded, shaking her head. "I don't feel good."

"Press that button," he said, pointing to a red switch on her side table. "That will alert the staff. I'm sure someone will be here soon to attend to you."

Tish winced as she bent to find the button before mouthing "Thank you," to Eli and lying flat on the bed to continue staring at the ceiling as she waited for help to come.

Chapter Two

The last thing Tish remembered before she woke up on the hospital bed was staring at herself in the mirror the morning after Adam arrived at the apartment. Even the memory of that was now hazy. Her image in the mirror when she regained consciousness at the apartment had seemed to belong to a different person, one who had been out of touch for days.

"How long have I been here?" she said to no one in particular as she waited for the nurse or doctor to appear. Her voice was rasp and loud enough to cause Jesse to stir and open her eyes. Her recollection of the events that put her in that hospital bed had jolted her idle memory and caused her to become more agitated than she was when she first opened her eyes.

"I don't know. We came in two days ago," Jesse responded, pointing to herself and then at Eli, "You've been unconscious since we arrived. You were here before us."

"What do you mean by unconscious? Where is Adam?"

"We discharged him yesterday," a man in a long white coat announced as he stepped into the ward and headed straight for Tish's bedside, with the nurse walking behind him.

"Hello, I'm Doctor Jorge. Glad you finally opened your eyes. How are you feeling today?" he asked with a sing-song Spanish inflection, placing the back of his hand over her forehead and grimacing with concern.

Tish creased her brows, alarmed by the look on his face. "Hi. I'm Tish. Why am I here? What is wrong with me?" she asked, her heart pounding as she waited for him to respond.

"*Fiebre Alta,*" the doctor said in Spanish, prompting the nurse to jot frantically in her notepad as he bent towards Tish and took her hand before muttering, "High fever."

"No wonder I feel so terrible," Tish managed to say through chattering teeth. "My head hurts."

"We'll give you something for the headache and the fever. We've been monitoring you for days. Your friend Adam was so worried you were never going to get up. If the mystery caller had not dialed 911 when he did, only God knows what would have happened to the both of you in that apartment. Consider yourself lucky to be alive."

Tish was entranced as he spoke. His words, more importantly, his tone, spelled that something more sinister than she could ever imagine had occurred, but what it was, though, she could not tell. Despite her deteriorating physical and mental state, her instinct was intact. It moved her to consider her words carefully as her life, and that of Adam's could depend on it.

"Why am I here? What…What are we all doing here?" she finally mustered the courage to ask, her heart racing as she spoke.

"You need to calm yourself down," the doctor warned, putting her hand down and muttering something indecipherable to the nurse before he focused his attention on Tish again.

"You're all in the same boat," he finally said, gesturing with his hands. "I've examined the others and run some tests. All four of you have been victims of some kind of medical foul play."

"Medical foul play?" Tish exclaimed, glaring wildly across the room as the rest of the patients, including Eli, and Jesse, looked on in anticipation. "I don't understand. Can you tell me more?"

"Well," the doctor continued. "From what I hear, there were unexplained noises in your accommodation, which might indicate you were being monitored. Whoever was responsible for this had access to your rooms while you slept. They took advantage of the situation and did things I doubt you approved of. From all I've seen, we're dealing with a severe case of malpractice. It's also important to keep in mind that these misdeeds may not have been carried out by registered professionals, which makes your case even more treacherous."

"What exactly did they do to me?" Tish muttered, running her hand across her chest once more. A strip of bandage lay along the path where she had seen the scar in the mirror the day she collapsed in front of the apartment's bathroom mirror.

"We have alerted the police here and contacted your family in the States," the doctor responded after hesitating for a few seconds. "The FBI may get involved at some point. Everyone is doing all they can with the investigation to figure out who did these things to you."

Tish's chest heaved frantically as the doctor spoke. "So, what did they do?" she asked again.

The doctor sighed and shook his head slowly before responding. "You received a heart transplant," he said, checking her pulse as he waited for what he'd just said to sink in.

"A heart what?" Tish shrieked, glancing around as if looking for support or maybe an affirmation of the seriousness of the emotional turmoil she had just been thrown into by the doctor's revelation.

"Yes, these people performed a heart transplant on you," the doctor repeated. "I want to plead with you to take things easy. Reacting this way will cause you more harm than good."

"How? Why?" Tish continued, flailing her hands and ignoring his warnings. "There was nothing wrong with my heart. What do you mean?"

"As I said earlier, there has been some kind of foul play. Do you remember revealing health problems of any kind to the organizers of this contest?"

"Why? No!" Tish yelled, wide-eyed and confused. "I have never ever been sick a day in my life, at least not since I was a kid. The last time I was in a hospital I was maybe seven or eight and it was to remove an abscess from my back. I don't recall entering that information in the form. I have even completely forgotten about that hospital stay until now."

"Are you sure? The others mentioned a contract. Just like you, none of them could remember agreeing to this. Do you really not recall anything? Do you remember signing any waivers?"

"I am very sure. What about the others? What did they do to them?"

"Doctor-patient confidentiality. I can't reveal more than I already did about the others to you. As I said earlier, the investigators are doing their work. You were all severely tampered with under the most bizarre circumstances. That's all I can tell you now."

The doctor's words sent shivers down her spine. She could feel her chest tighten as she thought back to the contract she'd signed. She was so desperate to leave her old world behind that she had signed whatever was put in front of her, without even reading the fine print. Now, it seemed that she had given away more than just her privacy for a prize that was turning out to be a nightmare. The pain in her chest grew stronger, and she couldn't help but feel angry at herself for not paying attention. Tears streamed down her face as she thought about the consequences of her actions. She knew she had to stay strong, but as the pain in her chest grew more intense, she couldn't help but wonder what else she had given away in those contracts.

"What of Adam?" she mustered the strength to ask.

Your boyfriend Adam was lucky. He recovered faster than every one of you."

"When can I see him?" she said in a pleading tone.

"Adam has been by your side since you got here. He refused to leave even after he was discharged and insisted on waiting for you to wake up. We had to force him to leave to get some food and a change of clothes."

"So when can I see him?" Tish persisted.

"Remember your promise to stay calm," the doctor said after hesitating for a second. We don't want you to relapse. In fact, you can't afford to. It could be deadly. We have to make sure you're stable before we introduce anything that will excite you. I need to attend to my other patients urgently. You're in good hands with the nurse. She'll check your vitals and we'll decide if the time is right to get these off you," he concluded, pointing to the tubes connected to various parts of her body, one to her arm and the others to her leg and stomach.

While the nurse strapped a sphygmomanometer to Tish's hand, she turned to Jesse. "I'm confused. Why are you and your…"

"My husband…I'm Jesse and he's Eli."

"Nice to meet you," Eli said, nodding in Tish's direction.

"Nice to meet you both," Tish responded. I saw the two of you the day I arrived at the apartment complex."

"I thought I saw someone that looked like you too," Jesse confirmed. "I was telling Eli that I recognized your face after we saw you lying there. There's no mistaking that red hair of yours. Even though you were black and blue when we arrived, I could still tell it was you because of the hair. It's beautiful."

"Thank you," Tish responded, running her free hand through her hair as a smile passed her lips. The thought that some part of her remained intact through her ordeal was enough to elicit that reaction. "Why are you both here? The doctor hinted at something. Did you also receive heart transplants? Were you—"

"Yeah," Eli responded, nodding before she could finish her sentence. We also received heart transplants out of nowhere. If you're wondering if we needed new hearts, wonder no more. We're in as much shock as you."

"My question is though, whose hearts and how?" Tish asked, but the nurse urged her to rest while she adjusted her blanket.

"We wish we knew the answer to that question," Eli said after the nurse left the ward. "They're currently investigating to find out exactly what happened. The speculation is that the contract we signed contained fine print that allowed our hosts access to our medical information and the power to do everything required to maintain our overall health."

"So I heard," Tish added.

"I wish we had paid attention to the fine print in those damn contracts," Jesse continued. "I feel like a stupid idiot right now."

Tish shook her head. "Same here. I'm so confused and…so upset at myself. I didn't stop to think before signing those papers. But how could we have known we would find ourselves in such a situation?"

"If we had used our brains from the beginning, we would have paid more attention to the fine print," Jesse echoed. "Speaking for myself, all I could see was an opportunity to have a great time and maybe rekindle my relationship with Eli. I honestly don't know what I was thinking when I signed up for this because it's unlike me to welcome everything that dangles its tail in front of me without doing some due diligence to understand its true origin. This time around, I don't know what came over me. The worst part is that I dragged Eli into this."

Eli hummed in discomfort. "Stop blaming yourself, Jesse. There's no way you would have known what was going on in these people's minds. If anything could have been done to prevent this, I know you, out of anyone else in this world, would have done that. You're very detailed and meticulous. Nothing passes by you."

"Exactly my point Eli," Jesse sobbed. "It completely went over my head."

"Stop it," Eli demanded. "You couldn't have known there was more to this than you signed up for. We just have to figure out how to get out of this nightmare. And we can't achieve that by laying blame."

Tish watched as Eli and Jesse interacted. She was taken aback by how kind and understanding Eli was to Jesse under such terrible circumstances. It was a far cry from how Eli had treated Jesse and herself when they had run into each other at the apartment complex the other day. To her, it seemed Eli was fully aware that Jesse was to blame for the mess they had found themselves in, but Eli didn't want her to feel guilty. He wanted to protect her. She couldn't help but feel a pang of jealousy towards Jesse. It was obvious that Eli loved her.

"So, what do we do now?" Tish asked after an awkward silence. "I want to go home!"

"We all want to go home," Jesse said, prompting a nod from Eli. "We all feel the same, but until we receive a full discharge from this hospital, I don't see how that's possible. These were serious procedures they carried out on us. We're kind of stuck here until we've fully recovered. I don't think we have much say in the matter."

"Has anyone tried to call Ty?" Tish asked after hesitating for a second.

Eli scoffed while Jesse shook her head before letting out a long sigh.

"Well, has anyone?" Tish repeated glaring in anticipation.

A long silence followed as Tish slowly moved her gaze from Jesse to Eli while she waited for one of them to volunteer a valid response. Eli was the first to speak. "Listen," he started. "Ty seems to have disappeared from the face of the earth. Thanks to your Adam with his photographic memory he remembered Ty's number when you got here. The hospital staff called him so many times but there was no response. They even sent a member of staff to the airport to investigate, but he returned with the report that no one had ever heard about Ty and Tidal Tours until then. You can't imagine how surprised we were when we received that news. We've tried everything we could but nothing has yielded results. Maybe Adam can tell you more about your particular situation. Your experience may be different from ours."

"I never trusted that Ty!" Tish exclaimed after Eli concluded his speech. "I just didn't think things could get this bad."

Jesse grimaced as she replied, "I had no reason to distrust him. What did he do to you?"

"Nothing specifically. He was a bit abrupt on one occasion. Oh, and he refused to answer when I called him to report this awful sound in the room after he specifically stated I could reach him anytime."

"You heard the sound too?" Jesse asked wide-eyed.

"Yes," Tish said, nodding. "It was awful."

"It was," Jesse agreed. "At first I thought it was nothing, but when Eli, who usually doesn't get bothered about things, sounded agitated when this eerie noise woke us up in the middle of the night, I began to get a little concerned myself. After I tried to appease him without luck, I called Ty, and he didn't pick up. That night, I ran to the lobby and tried to reach him through the hotel phone, but he also didn't answer. As I was about to call Tidal Tours, I thought I saw someone who looked like Ty dropping a woman off in the same limousine he picked us up in, but by the time I ran out to confront him, after hesitating a bit as I only had a robe on, he had driven off."

"When was this?" Tish blurted. "When did all this happen?"

"That was the day I arrived. The same day Eli and I bumped into you. I later tried his number several times when we got up in the morning, and it just rang engaged. I haven't heard from him since then."

Chapter Three

Tish's heart raced with excitement as Adam hobbled towards her bedside, his eyes sparkling with joy as he saw her eyes light up at the sight of him. Despite leaning on a walking stick for support, he still exuded charm and seemed genuinely happy to see Tish wide awake.

"Adam," she cried, attempting to raise her head as he bent down to kiss her,

grabbing his chest as he grunted in pain.

Tish watched as he struggled to catch his breath with the slightest movement. "Sit down," she pleaded. She couldn't bear to see him suffer.

"Hello, Tish," he whispered, sitting on the edge of the bed. He held her up gently to plant another kiss on her lips, easing her pain as his warmth flowed through her. She closed her eyes and basked in the feeling of being cared for and loved. When he finally released her, he took her right hand and squeezed it so hard as though fearing this reality would be over if he as much as entertained the thought of letting go.

"Hi Adam," Tish responded, gazing into his eyes. "I thought I'd lost you. I really thought—"

"Shh!" Adam interjected, placing his index finger on her lip. "I missed you, Tish. I love you," he said, just loud enough for her to hear.

Tears rolled down Tish's eyes. "I love you too," she mumbled.

"Can you repeat what you just said?" Adam pleaded, leaning forward.

"I said, I love you too."

Adam heaved a huge sigh of relief, placing one hand over his chest. He turned to look around the room, but everyone seemed to be minding their business, so he returned his attention to Tish. The ward was filled with a deafening silence, so quiet, you could hear a pin drop. Yet, it was nothing compared to the pounding of Adam's heart, which seemed to echo throughout the room. The stillness was suffocating like a thick fog had descended upon the space. It was as if the entire room was holding its breath, waiting for the next beat.

"Did you mean what you just said?" Adam asked in a monotone when he finally spoke.

"Of course I did. From the bottom of my heart." Tish smiled; her shyness evident in the way she chuckled as she glanced around the room fully aware that they were not alone.

Adam's lips parted, a gasp escaping them as he gazed at Tish in awe. His eyes widened as he took in every detail of her, from her soft features to the way her hair fell perfectly around her face. He couldn't deny how he felt, and hearing her words sent him over the moon. Confusion flooded Adam's expression as he sighed and shook his head in disbelief. His leg shuffled back and forth, a clear sign of his nervousness. Despite his astonishment, a happy smile remained plastered on his face. Tish's words had left him in a state of pure joy and he couldn't help but show it.

"You've turned so pale, Adam," Tish said, slightly concerned as she gently caressed his chin with her free hand. "You look like you've just seen a ghost.".

"I'm in shock. That's all," he said, placing his hand over hers and softly kissing the corners of her pinky finger. "I wish things would always remain as they are at this moment."

"Why are you so shocked?"

"Why?" he said, gazing at her in disbelief, his eyes reflecting the hurt and longing that had been hidden for so long. "Because I have loved you since the day I set my eyes on you, and I dared not confess that to you before now as you had outrightly rejected me. I never in a million years imagined you would fall in love with me for real. That's why I'm shocked. I don't know how to handle this."

His words were spoken with such sincerity, finally revealing his truth. Adam couldn't believe that Tish had fallen for him after all this time. He continued to stare at her, his heart pounding with a mix of emotions. The memories of their exchanges on their Q phones now seemed insignificant. It was a dream come true, and he couldn't believe it was happening. He was captivated by her beauty, her words, and the love she exuded.

"I liked you the first day I met you, although for obvious reasons I couldn't act on that," Tish assured him. "I liked you when we played on those phones. I started liking you a little more the night we hung out at the club, but what I feel now is much different. It trumps everything that came before that. Does that make sense? Because it doesn't make sense to me."

"That exercise with our Q phones was more than a game to me," Adam responded, shaking his head. "Whether we like it or not, the shit worked, because, by the time they asked us to submit the phones, I honestly believed you were as much in love with me as I was with you. Sounds like you only liked me."

"Erm…" Tish mumbled, raising her brows and crinkling her nose as she contemplated how to answer to Adam's question. The truth was that she had not been invested as much, not as much as Adam was at that time, but she wasn't going to tell that to him. Revealing that now would serve no purpose, in her mind.

"In my opinion," Adam continued, after he received no response from her, "everything changed when you realized the guy you met on that lonely street in Long Island was the same person you'd been chatting with all these months. I was shocked to see you totally backtracked the day I arrived at the apartment. Your aloofness caught me off guard, so to admit that you love me now is something I never expected from you."

"Well…It's the first time I've felt like I love you," Tish confessed, peering into his eyes.

"What caused your change of heart?" Adam asked, breathing heavily.

Tish shrugged. "I don't know. Does it need any explanation?"

"It seems sudden to me."

"Hmm. Yes, maybe. I agree," Tish said, raising her brows and bobbing her head. "I can't explain why my feelings changed drastically. It just happened. Maybe when I get out of this bed and actually have some time to dissect everything that's happened so far, including what got me here in the first place, I can begin to make sense of it. For now, I just want to live in the moment. Is that too much to ask?"

Adam and Tish went back and forth about their feelings for each other completely unaware of everyone else around them. Jesse, Eli, the other patients, and their visitors watched their entire exchange in awe. Eli's Adam's apple bulged as he stole a glance at Jesse. The free declaration of love and affection had ignited strong feelings inside of him. It was difficult to hide what he felt for Jesse at that moment. A tear welled up in Jesse's eye, betraying the flood of emotions that surged within. The realization of unspoken feelings, the longing that had been carefully tucked away, rose to the surface. Jesse's hand trembled as it reached up to wipe away the solitary tear that escaped, a silent witness to the emotional storm brewing within.

Tish only realized that everyone was staring at them after the doctor cleared his throat as he entered the ward. She covered her mouth with one hand and eyed him furtively before shifting her glance around, willing the spectators to give her and Adam the privacy they desperately desired. But it was too late. Everyone now knew their business and the depth of their affection for each other. The doctor smiled while he completed his examination and jotted notes on his pad before hurriedly excusing himself from the room.

Tish hated being the center of attention like she found herself at that moment. Her cheeks flushed with embarrassment. Adam did not care if the whole world was watching.

"I am so in love with you," he declared to Tish after the doctor left. "You won't believe it, but I sat in this position and stared at you for three days straight after I was allowed to leave my bed. If they hadn't forced me to take a break, I would have been by your side when you woke up. I regret that I wasn't there."

"Three days!" Tish exclaimed, glaring at him. "Did you say you sat here for three days? How long have I been unconscious?"

"We arrived here ten days ago."

"Oh my God!" Tish squealed.

"What is it, Tish? What happened?"

"I can't believe I've been here this long," Tish said agitatedly, shaking her head, her chest heaving up and down.

"Take it easy," Adam pleaded. "I don't want the nurse or the doctor to come running in here. They'll think you've suffered a relapse and try to sedate you again. Please try to stay calm, and yes, it's been ten days since you collapsed in that bugged apartment."

"I don't believe it, Adam…Are you telling me that it's been over ten days since we went to dinner and the club?"

Adam sighed and rubbed his neck before muttering, "It's been longer than that. It's been fifteen days since that night. We spent a few days at the apartment after the unfortunate incidents that brought us here. We woke up some days later."

Tish swallowed hard as Adam's revelation hit her like a ton of bricks. His words echoed and faded with each rise and fall of her chest. She gasped in hopes of averting the sudden pain that gripped her insides before grabbing

Adam's arm. "Did you say fifteen?" she mumbled, tears rolling down her eyes.

"I'm sorry, Tish."

"I just want to go home. My family must be worried about me now. Take me home now!"

"The doctor has assured us all they're working on getting us home. Quit acting this way, or he'll return and sedate you," Adam pleaded. "You need to be as alert as possible for us to work through this. We all do. I only have myself to blame for not taking things seriously when you pointed out those weird sounds in the apartment. If I had listened to you when you insisted something was wrong, we would not be in this position. I'm a fool for disregarding your concerns, not to mention the fact that I dragged you into this horrible experiment. I would never have imagined it would lead to this. Do you believe me?"

"I don't know what to believe, but I'll try my best to stay calm," she said, still sobbing.

"I'm so sorry for putting you through this, Tish. I'll spend the rest of my life trying to make this up to you. I swear, I will."

"Stop swearing Adam. And stop apologizing. You could not have known the contest organizers would have the mind to do these things when you signed up for the experiment. None of us could have known. Before you came in, I was speaking to Eli and Jesse about the contest and how they lied to us. We were all conned. And the worst part is we still don't know the full extent of the prize we have to pay. Isn't it ironic that we came to receive a prize, yet from everything we've witnessed so far, it seems we're the prize?"

"So you believe I had nothing to do with this?"

"Why would you knowingly put yourself in this type of position?"

"Tish, you don't know how happy it makes me to hear you say that. I'm now convinced we can get through this together. There's something I wanted to ask you…Have you noticed something strange?" he said tightening his lips.

"Like what?" Tish asked, aghast.

"Do you feel different inside?"

"How do you mean?"

"I feel as though something messed with my head. I no longer feel like myself. What about you? Are you okay?"

Tish shook her head in exasperation. "You're speaking in riddles, Adam. I don't understand what you mean."

Adam paused for a few seconds before continuing. "How can I explain this?" he asked rhetorically. "Let's just say that I now worry about every damn thing. Excuse my language, but it's gotten so bad that I find myself worrying about ridiculous things that are yet to happen in the future. Before now, I never gave a damn about anything, except you."

"What type of things," Tish asked, wiping the tears from her face with the corner of her blanket.

"Oh. Things that never used to cross my mind. Marriage for instance. Recently, I have been thinking about children, retirement, and even death. Is that normal?"

"I used to think all that was normal," Tish blurted, a smile slanting the corner of her lips. "That used to be my thing."

"Used to?" Adam asked in surprise.

"Yes. I no longer see myself as that person," Tish continued. "Is it strange that all I care about right now is that I love you and that I want to go home?"

"I love you too, but don't you want to find out how you got here?" Adam inquired.

"Well, yes, but will that change anything, though," Tish responded.

"Well…well—"

Adam let out a deep sigh, knowing that he had given this line of argument his best effort. He had never thought Tish would be so lackadaisical. It was unlike her to be so carefree. He had always admired her for her serious-mindedness and unwillingness to take things at face value. But now, she was adamant that she didn't care about anything else but getting home. *How was it possible that she had become this way?* He thought, feeling frustrated when he couldn't pinpoint the reason behind her change in mannerism.

"Adam. Adam," Tish called, bringing him back to earth.

Adam's eyes softened as he looked at her, but Tish noticed that Adam looked a little off. She had seen that look before, and it usually meant struggle with something. Ever since she woke up in the hospital, she had felt like she was living in someone else's shoes, so she could relate to his position of not feeling like himself anymore. Since she woke up in that hospital, she had been trying to make sense of it all, but it was a lot to take in alongside everything else she had been through. She had been so focused on the bodily harm that she hadn't stopped to appreciate the changes that had occurred on her inside. The more she thought about it, she couldn't help but wonder if there was more to her newfound view of the world.

Chapter Four

They were interrupted by the sound of the doctor's voice.

"We're closer to finding out what really happened," he announced, stepping into the ward with a pile of papers and a blank look on his face. "I have the results of some of the tests."

"What could be worse than what we already know?" Eli responded, sounding like a petulant teenager.

"Give me a moment to explain," the doctor retorted as Jesse, Tish, and Adam looked on with furrowed brows. Jesse clasped her shoulders with both hands as though trying to stop her heart from jumping out of her chest. "I knew something fishy was going on here but your hearts getting interchanged, was something I could never have imagined."

"What do you mean?" Eli and Adam asked in unison.

"It was clear by the nature of your injuries," the doctor continued, "that your hearts were tampered with.

What we could not easily determine was the extent of the interference."

"I don't—" Adam began to say, but the doctor raised both hands to placate him.

"Wait…Let me finish then you can ask questions…Okay? The four of you were in dreadful states when you arrived here. It was obvious by direct examination what was going on, but we were all surprised you were able to breathe on your own without the help of an apparatus."

"Is that not a good thing?" Adam asked, interrupting him again.

"Yes," the doctor responded. "As you already know, it meant the procedure was carried out several days before you arrived. Transplant patients usually cannot breathe without some sort of help. They need a breathing tube to survive for a few days, but all of you, except Tish, were breathing on your own without too much difficulty. Since we had zero knowledge of why or how you got the surgeries and even what type of care you received afterwards, we decided to investigate the matter a little bit. We needed more information so we could offer you the right treatment. The first step we took was to find out how the organs were procured. We thought that would be easy as heart transplants require artful coordination between the donor, the procurement organization, and the recipient's doctors. However, when our calls to the hospitals with the means to handle this type of case in the area proved futile, we realized something more sinister could be going on."

The doctor paused to scan the faces in the room. Except for Jesse, who grunted as she adjusted herself on the bed, everyone looked on in anticipation, eager for him to continue.

"Are you okay?" Eli asked Jesse, signaling to the doctor to check on her. "She looks paler than usual."

"Oh, I'm okay considering the circumstances," Jesse responded. "Please go on. Don't worry about me."

"The doctor glanced at Jesse. "Let me know if you need me to pause anytime," he said to before continuing. "After our investigation failed, we decided to try something that has existed for a while in the medical community but which we have never really put into practice. From recent medical research, we know that donor DNA could reside in the recipient's plasma due to some complicated phenomenon I don't think I could begin to explain right now. Borrowing from that study, we now know that Jesse and Tish received their male partner's hearts. Unfortunately, since this detection method only works if the donor is male, we cannot say with certainty whose hearts Eli and Adam have received."

You could hear a pin drop in the ward as the doctor stopped to gauge their reaction. All four of them seemed frozen to the spot, unable to speak. Moments later, Tish was gasping for breath, so the doctor rushed to her side and placed an oxygen mask over her face. Adam was the first to recover. "So, how can we find out whose hearts we received?" he asked, staring intently at the doctor.

"It's safe to assume you received your female partner's hearts. Now, though there is no way to prove that, it's safe to assume that Eli has Jesse's heart and Adam has Tish's. Considering how difficult it is to procure this vital organ even for patients in critical condition, this seems to be the most plausible position."

"How old is this research?" Adam asked. "I'm wondering why it can be used to determine what one gender received and not the other?"

"Something to do with the possibility of detection of Y chromosomes in the tissues of the female—" the doctor began to say before Adam countered.

"Is that enough to conclude that the women received our hearts? Could the Y chromosomes not belong to any male?"

"I just informed you that your heart was swapped," the doctor responded. "Shouldn't that be top of your mind now? Why do you care about the rest of the details? You're lucky you survived this ordeal. Let's focus on what's important for now."

"And what is that?" Adam asked.

"To get you all well enough to be on your way home. Any more questions before I leave?" the doctor asked impatiently.

An uncomfortable silence passed as all four of them looked at one another.

"Why would they do a thing like that? Why did they switch our hearts?" Jesse finally asked.

"That's what the authorities are still trying to find out," the doctor responded before retreating from the room, leaving his four patients looking on as though they had just seen a ghost.

Chapter Five

After a forty-minute drive, with some detours and wrong turns, the taxi driver found the tiny one-bedroom bungalow the hospital rented for them in Guanacaste two days after Tish was discharged. The hospital advised them to lay low while the police and the FBI completed their investigations and the embassy could issue their travel documents. In addition to their phones, their passports had failed to turn up in the apartment search conducted by the Public Force. To make calls to their friends and family, who had started to pool resources to see to their safe return home, they visited a convenience store about a three-kilometer drive from the bungalow.

Shortly after they arrived, they huddled around the small breakfast table in the living room and discussed how they could help the situation without obstructing the authorities. They had abandoned their personal effects in their old apartments, so they had little to work with. Those were now designated crime scenes and were no longer considered accessible or safe.

The sun had set on the horizon, casting a warm orange glow on the ocean. The familiar smell that once brought joy now brought a sense of melancholy. Through the open window, the kitchen was filled with the salty scent, bringing back memories of happier times. A distant rumble broke the silence, causing surprised stares around the table. The once clear blue sky was now turning a deep shade of purple. The sight was a stark reminder of the fleeting nature of happiness and how quickly things can change. Something they all knew too well.

"It's quite late, and I believe it'll be dangerous to go into the city right now," Eli said to no one in particular.

"For sure. Not in this weather," Adam responded. "It'll be better if we go tomorrow. We'll set out early, so we can be back in time just in case we need to leave ASAP. The embassy could be ready with our papers anytime from now."

"Be careful out there," Jesse said, rubbing Eli's back in a circular motion. "Tidal Tours may have sent their people to look for us. You never know what they have in mind. One of them may be lurking around the apartments, waiting to pounce when you least expect. We need to make sure we're not setting a trap for ourselves."

"You're right dear. We'll be careful when we go," Eli responded.

"Why don't we go in disguise?" Adam suggested. "That would throw anyone with evil plans off course. What do you all think?"

"That's a great idea," Tish agreed, nodding and smiling at Jesse. "Jesse and I can help you guys out."

They barely slept that night, their minds saddled with their coming adventure. The next day, Eli and Adam shaved their beards and swapped the clothes they were given at the hospital with t-shirts and khaki pants they had bought from the local market on their way to the bungalow the day before. Adam opted for a more demure look, donning non-prescription sunglasses that immediately transformed his image from a regular Playboy to a studious bookworm. Eli, on the other hand, went for a more youthful appearance, chopping off his shoulder-length hair and wearing a backward-facing baseball cap. True to their word, Tish and Jesse woke up early to help them perfect their disguises. Jesse expertly trimmed Eli's bushy eyebrows, leaving just enough to avoid suspicion. The snip successfully achieved the desired transformation. Tish then used makeup purchased from the market to create highlights that softened Eli's features. Meanwhile, using a different shade, she worked wonders on Adam's face, skillfully contouring his nose and concealing any dark circles under his eyes, giving him a more youthful and refreshed appearance.

While Tish and Jesse recovered at the bungalow, Eli and Adam combed through the city in search of anything or anyone that might know something, even if remote, about Ty and Tidal Tours. Their first port of call was the apartment complex. Situated in an area frequently visited by tourists and known to host several parties on its grounds, it was easy to locate. The reception desk was empty, but the lobby was buzzing with vacationers. Some were seated on stools in the café, speaking at the top of their voices, while others stood around in shorts or swimsuits, wet from an early morning swim at the nearby beach.

"It'll be a good idea for us to split up," Eli said to Adam while they waited for the receptionist to appear. "See what you can find out while I scope the area. We'll meet here in twenty minutes max. After that, we can decide what to do next."

"Sounds great," Adam responded. "See you in a bit."

A few minutes after Eli left, a man in a white uniform and a white face cap appeared at the counter.

"Good morning," Adam said casually, cautious to avoid giving the impression that he was there for anything other than to inquire about accommodation.

"Good morning," the man responded in a somber tone. "Sorry for keeping you waiting."

"No worries. Do you have any rooms available?" Adam asked.

"Yes, always. What type of room do you need? We have some two-bedroom apartments available. We've also had recent vacancies for our studio apartments, but those will not be available until next week," the man said.

"How so?"

"The accident—" he started to say and was interrupted by a woman's voice calling him from somewhere behind the counter. "Excuse me," he said, waving before walking away.

Two minutes later, a short woman in her thirties appeared. Without so much as a hello, she announced that she had one and two bedrooms available. "What are you looking for?" she asked Adam, her eyes fixed on him as she waited for a response.

"How much is the one bedroom?" Adam asked to avert suspicion as he pondered the man's sudden disappearance while the woman continued to question him about his preferences. He thought it bizarre that the man suddenly vanished and considered asking the woman if he could speak with the man instead, but realized that would draw unnecessary attention. Their old accommodations were studio apartments, and their rooms had been right across from each other. This had given the perpetrators easy access to perform the dastardly acts they did to them.

"Eight hundred," the woman responded.

"What about the two bedrooms? Can we see one before we commit?" Adam asked, sounding non-committal.

"The two bedrooms are sixteen hundred, but I'm short-staffed right now. I can call you to view them once I have someone available to show them to you. Will you be interested in a call?"

"Can the man show me?" he requested, throwing caution to the wind by ignoring her request. He decided to focus on what was top of his mind regardless of the added danger of drawing attention to himself and potentially blowing his cover.

"Which man?" the woman asked, glancing behind her.

"The one I was just speaking with. In the white uniform."

"He doesn't work here. He was just filling in for someone. Would you like to get a call?" she repeated, peering into his eyes.

Adam carefully contemplated his next statement and decided it was better to play safe. "What floor are those on?" he asked nonchalantly.

"Second."

"Any spots on the fifth floor?" he asked, hoping the woman would release information that would help his investigation as they had been on the fifth floor during their stay.

"No, sir," she responded in a casual tone, making it difficult for Adam to detect if she had something to hide.

Chapter Six

As Adam handled the receptionist, Eli roamed the premises, engaging in conversations and pausing intermittently to inquire about Ty's whereabouts. Despite his attempts to sound inconspicuous, his untrained acting abilities garnered attention from onlookers. Some of the workers in uniform became cautious of his questions and divulged less information than they had in their possession. In the end, no one he spoke to admitted to knowing anyone by the name Ty nor by the description that was provided. One thing he got from the interactions was that some programming had convinced the residents of the need to distance themselves from potentially hazardous situations.

Since Adam had time to kill after dealing with the receptionist, he hung around the lobby, hoping Eli would return on time before his presence started to arouse suspicion. Forty minutes after they were supposed to have met, Adam headed out to find Eli. The sun's rays were in his eyes, but from a distance, he could make out Eli sprinting in the direction of the building, waving frantically and yelling at the top of his voice. Adam dashed to meet him, but Eli suddenly stopped some seconds later, placing both hands on his legs as he struggled to catch some air. Some bystanders started to gather around him, seemingly out of concern, but he stood upright just as Adam approached. The small crowd slowly dispersed, muttering amongst themselves, some shaking their heads in disdain.

"Did you see him?" he said to Adam, breathing heavily.

"Did I see whom?" Adam asked, shaking his head. "What happened? You're drawing so much attention to yourself…To us. I thought we agreed to—"

"Did you see Ty?" Eli repeated.

"No," Adam said. "I talked to the receptionist and—"

"Are you telling me you didn't see Ty or someone that looks like Ty running in that direction?" Eli continued in a frantic tone, pointing towards the building. "Nothing?" He asked again, lowering his voice so no one would overhear him.

"Nothing!" Adam responded. "Are you sure it was him?"

"I could swear then it was him. I can't be so sure now, as I only saw this guy's back. If only you had come out earlier, you might have seen him walking towards the building."

"He entered the building?" Adam asked, taking a moment to glance behind him mouth agape.

"I think so," Eli answered dejectedly. "Now, I'm not sure who that was."

"I'm so sorry, Eli. When I saw you running, creating a scene, all I wanted to do was to get to you to make you stop. I didn't think of checking out the people in the background. If Ty had barged into me at that moment, I'm sure I wouldn't have noticed. There's no time to waste. We should immediately check the building before he leaves. Hurry!"

He turned and walked stealthily in the direction of the building, and Eli followed him. Moving in opposite directions, they quickly scanned the lobby, converging a few seconds later with forlorn looks on their faces. After their search produced no results, they hatched a plan to sneak upstairs to the fifth floor to see if they could access their old apartments. The only option available for bypassing security cameras in the elevator was to take the stairs. They rounded the corner and found the entrance to the staircase. The landing was clear. Eli took one step and gave Adam a sign to join him.

Together, they climbed several flights until they got to the landing of the fifth floor. The floor had been cordoned off, and two uniformed security men were guarding the area. Signs read *"No hay entrada,"* but they continued walking with a spring in their step, as though the rules did not apply to them. Just as they bent down to sneak under the ribbons, one of the security men placed a hand on Eli's shoulder, stopping them in their tracks.

"Hey, you're not supposed to go in there. What do you want?" the man grilled them in Spanish.

"What floor is this?" Adam asked, pretending to have missed his way.

The man pointed at the number five on the wall. "The fifth," he said.

"Oh. Sorry," Adam said as they both stepped back before quietly retreating and trotting down the stairs.

"What do we do now?" Eli asked Adam after they got to the ground floor. "We can't get past those men. Maybe we should walk a bit and come back later. They can't guard that floor twenty-four seven."

"I don't think we'll find the answer we're looking for here," Adam said. "Did you take a good look at those men? They would have eaten us alive if we didn't do what they asked. By the way, the receptionist appeared after you left to search the grounds. He was about to tell me something, but he disappeared when a woman came out of nowhere. I feel he knows something about the contest."

"Suppose we bribe them. Do you think that'll work?" Eli asked.

"We can try, but that will make us seem desperate and even more suspicious. We've already done a poor job at staying under the radar, and as you can see, there are security men everywhere."

"Yeah. I noticed," Eli said, looking around. "What should we do now? Should we try to speak to him again?"

"What have we got to lose?" Adam said, shrugging his shoulders.

When they arrived at the lobby and the man was still not there, it became clear to both of them after ten minutes of waiting that there would be no answer at the apartment complex. With only a few hours to spare, they decided to comb the city for tips and return in the evening with hopes of sighting Ty. With all the information at their fingertips, they both felt it was unlikely Ty would be roaming around in broad daylight. He was their number one suspect, and it was more probable that he would operate at night, if at all.

Chapter Seven

Around noon, Adam and Eli left the apartments and decided to visit bars around the city. In their inquiries, they described Ty as young, about twenty-something or early thirties, slim. He could be Costa Rican, Nicaraguan or Panamanian. A good-looking man, they always indicated but with no distinct facial features to go by. It was a tricky task for them as they did not have an actual picture of Ty to work with. A sketch was out of the way as neither one of them knew how to draw. The Love Experiment website had disappeared since their ordeal began, and the number provided by Tidal Tours in Boston no longer existed. They had all agreed a long time ago that all that had been a sham. After several failed attempts, half smiles, some snickering behind their backs, and some voices with genuine concern, about halfway through the day, they both concluded the name Ty was a cover, and Ty, as they knew him, never really existed.

Around four in the afternoon, they eventually decided to give themselves a break and grab a bite to eat. Without prior knowledge of the area, they settled on the first local joint they saw with two seats open. After stuffing themselves and chatting for a good while to allow time for their food to settle, they decided to visit a discotheque on the east end of town to relax and grab some drinks.

"I think we should call it a day now," Adam said to Eli as they hovered over their beer glasses. "Tish and Jesse will be worried about us. "We've left them alone for too long."

"I agree. We should head back once we finish our drinks," Eli responded. "I wonder what they've been up to. Our lives have been torturous recently. It'll be terrible if we have to make them worry about us on top of it all."

Despite tirelessly scouring, their quest yielded no results. Instead of receiving concern, they were given suspicious glances and disdainful stares from those who couldn't fathom how rational individuals could find themselves in such a chaotic situation.

"Torturous is an understatement. And today has been a huge disappointment," Adam agreed. "This whole situation has taken a huge toll on my mind. I can't believe how drastically things have changed for me."

"What do you mean," Eli asked.

"I don't know how to explain this. The extent of worry that passes through me daily is something completely foreign to me."

"Chronic worrying?" Eli interjected, shuffling his feet and nodding his head repeatedly. "We're in the same boat. Since the transplant, I've been worrying nonstop, much like how Jesse would have behaved given the same set of circumstances. I used to be so relaxed. I let her do everything, worry about the bills, and our future, even if the relationship was going to work. She even set this shit up. She agreed to this arrangement to make sure we've given our relationship its best shot. Now, see how the tides have turned. I'm the one trying to fix everything and even though that seems like the only thing to do, this new way of being has made me severely unhappy, or should I say seriously depressed. No matter how hard I try I can't shake this terrible feeling…"

His voice cracked, and he threw his head back and fought back tears while Adam tapped him lightly on the arm to calm him.

"I'm happy we got to talk about this," Adam said. "I've experienced the exact same things you just described. In the little time I've known Tish, she's taken most of the lead in investigating the little things like the weird noise in the apartment the day I arrived. Don't get me wrong. I no longer consider that a little thing. But Tish…She was so sure the beep was something and I played it down. Now, I'm the one worrying about every little thing, including whatever we may have left behind in the apartment, and all she cares about is going home. I hate that the rooms were blockaded. The way I feel right now, I want to go in there and comb through every inch of it until I discover something that could expose these criminals. I have a strong feeling that the people carrying out this investigation are doing a shitty job."

"My sentiment also."

"You know what else? I have never been more in love with Tish than I am right now."

"Damn! You took the words right out of my mouth!" Eli exclaimed. "I was going to say that about Jesse. I was so excited to leave Boston and come to Costa Rica to get as far away from her as possible but look at me now. I'm head over heels in love with her."

"I've noticed the way you look at her. I also observed that whenever she glances at you, you suddenly avert your gaze and start doing something else."

"Like what?" Eli asked.

"Anything other than what is expected of you in that moment. It's rather pretentious. What's up with that?" Adam asked, shaking his head. "When were you planning to tell her exactly how you feel?"

"Was I that obvious?" Eli asked, chuckling. "What can I say? I'm an open book. Do you think she notices?"

"The most clueless of persons would have noticed. I'm not sure she would have, though. You know what they say about the victim being the last to know. I think you should tell her soon. We could all have died from this ordeal. Tell her now before it's too late."

Eli scratched his head and sighed. "It's the worrying thing I told you about. I've ignored her for so long. Now, I just fear it might be too late to turn things around."

"You never know unless you try," Adam insisted.

"I know her too well," Eli continued. "She's the type to get suspicious and laugh in my face if I suddenly declare my love for her. That response could break my already fragile heart to pieces."

At the mention of heart, Adam pushed his half-empty jug away and pressed his temple with both hands. "Wait…Are you thinking what I'm thinking?" he asked, staring intently at Eli.

"I believe so?" Eli said with a look of confusion on his face.

"Could the sole purpose of the transplant be to push us into falling in love with one another?" Adam asked, stepping down from his stool, while continuing to stare at Eli, his chest heaving up and down as he waited for Eli to concur. "I mean, it's not called the 'Love Experiment' for nothing. Tish loves me very much now. She told me so when she woke up at the hospital. As for me, I now love her more than I love myself. No…I now love her more than life itself."

Eli dismounted from his stool and folded his hands across his chest, panting as the pensive look on his face slowly turned to terror. "What do we do now?" He asked no one in particular.

"First things first," Adam responded. "Let's find out if Jesse feels the same way about you."

"Could Jesse love me like I love her now?" Eli asked, fear and excitement rising in his voice.

"What do you think?"

"What do I think?" Eli repeated, casting him a roguish glance. "I can't wait to find out."

Take Me Home Now
Book Four

Chapter One

"FBI. Special agent Mark Drummonds," the burly man in plainclothes announced, flashing a badge after Adam answered a frantic knock on the door. "We're here to transport you to a safe house."

"What for?" Adam asked, shooting a glance over Agent Drummonds' shoulder.

"We've received instructions to take you somewhere more secure while the embassy sorts out your documents," he responded.

"ID please," Adam said, stretching out his hand. After their experience the day before combing through Guanacaste looking for any clue that would expose the criminals that bastardized their bodies, he didn't think any precaution was exorbitant.

"Of course," the agent nodded, pulling a card from his breast pocket and handing it to him.

Adam inspected the card closely. The name was the same, but the image appeared to be that of a much younger man, a version of the person standing before him. "It's the FBI," he yelled as Eli approached, with Tish and Jesse trailing behind him.

"Are our papers ready?" Eli inquired as he shook Agent Drummonds' hand.

"Look," the agent continued with a sense of urgency, "We don't have time for questions. You're not safe here. They're watching you."

"Who's watching us?"

Agent Drummonds clenched his teeth in a grimace. "What do you think?" he asked, staring at Eli. "The same people who did these things to you. We need to get out of here. Quickly everyone!"

The sound of his voice left the four of them with no choice but to scuttle around the bungalow to pack their few belongings before converging in a black van parked at the rear entrance. A uniformed police officer stood outside and waited for them to enter before positioning himself beside the driver and the front row. Agent Drummonds sat with Eli and Jesse at the back, while Adam and Tish settled in the middle.

"What happens now?" Adam asked in a frantic tone, still dazed by the manner they were ushered out of the bungalow, without so much as a clue as to where they were going. "We just need to go home. I spoke to the embassy yesterday and our travel documents will be ready tomorrow."

"Yes, but you're in severe danger right now," the agent said, pulling out a few sheets of paper from a large envelope as he signaled the driver to move. He tapped Adam on the shoulder and handed him the papers.

Adam took one look and gasped. "I don't understand. What's going on here?"

"Can I," Eli said, reaching out to grab the sheets from Adam.

"Just a second," Adam said, leafing through the rest of the pages before handing them to Eli.

"What the heck is this?" Eli asked as he looked through the papers with Jesse.

Each sheet contained close personal images of the couples in various states on the property, at the club, at the phone booth, and even in the backyard of the small bungalow. One of the images was of Tish and Jesse stepping out on the porch for a few minutes the day before. Another was of Eli and Adam in the discotheque. A couple more were of them speaking to different people in the city. Jesse's jaw dropped when she got to one where she was resting on Eli's lap, half-dressed in the backyard as he consoled her and professed his love to her, a moment so sacred, it was impossible to believe it had been penetrated by a foreign party.

"Do you all now see what I mean when I say you can't be here a second longer? You're still a target for these people. Their snipers have guns pointed at your heads at every point in time."

At the mention of guns, Tish started to sob while Adam gently caressed her shoulders. All the blood had drained from Jesse's face. She was frozen to the spot, unable to speak or move.

Eli was the only one with some semblance of control. "These people seem to be monitoring our every move. We believed we were out of the danger zone since the police and the FBI were now involved. When will this nightmare be over?" he asked.

"You can never be completely safe until you leave this region. Do you understand that?" Agent Drummonds responded, glaring at him.

"I think we can all agree to that by now," Eli said defeatedly. "How did you get these photos?"

Agent Drummonds hesitated a bit before responding. "Someone faxed them to one of our associates last night. We're still trying to trace its source. It's definitely a warning."

"Is wherever we're headed any safer? How do we know when we're out of danger?"

"It is, or we would not have been taking you there."

Eli continued to question Agent Drummonds as the van zipped through the dirt roads and merged into the busy city traffic, where it slowed and then maneuvered its way until they reached the highway.

"Don't freak out about what I'm about to tell you," Agent Drummonds warned after they had driven almost ten minutes on the highway. "This is not the first case of this type we've had to deal with. But before I get into that, I need to ask you all a question. Have you ever wondered what happened to the other contestants?"

"Which ones?" Adam asked.

"Don't tell me you've already forgotten there were supposed to be eight 'lucky' winners," Agent Drummonds said, making an air quote by holding his index and middle fingers upward and bending them toward his palms at the mention of the word lucky. "Did you think the four of you were the only ones in this predicament?"

"That's true. They told us about eight winners, but we haven't heard of the others," Adam confirmed. "Where are they?"

"Well," Agent Drummonds said, shaking his head slowly. "Contestants five six seven eight or as they like to call them, 105, 106, 107, 108, have all been murdered."

"Murdered? How?" Jesse asked, her heart beating uncontrollably as her mind flew to the woman she saw with Ty the night she came down to the lobby to a call, wondering if she was one of the victims and wishing she had got the chance to warn her.

"They didn't survive the operation. I wouldn't be surprised if they tried to do away with you to cover up everything. That might be why they're watching so closely to ensure you don't escape."

A sudden chill spread across the van that had begun to get stuffy after thirty minutes of driving at full speed on the highway. Through their travails, they had forgotten about the other contestants, but no one could blame them when they found themselves in positions where they had to fight for their lives and had no visibility into the fate of the others. Ty had made that fact clear in the beginning. That the four of them met was sheer coincidence, one that the contest organizers would have frowned at.

"How do we know they're not after us right now?" Tish asked after she recovered from her initial shock.

"Don't worry, you're safe with us. Once we get you to a safe location, we'll remove the chips they're using to monitor you. As we speak, these criminals can read your temperature, reactions, words, and even your heartbeat. We have to extract the chips from where they've been implanted so you can finally be free of them."

"They implanted chips inside our bodies? What part?" Adam asked in a distressing tone.

"We don't know. The doctor will locate and remove them," Agent Drummonds responded.

"I don't believe this," Adam said. "I hope it's not at the site of the surgery."

"It's a microchip. They could have inserted it into any part of the body. These types of things are common these days. An X-ray will easily identify the location so we can extract it. I wouldn't worry too much about it," Agent Drummonds assured them.

"Are you sure they can't track our location right now? Are we completely safe with you?" Eli asked.

"You have nothing to worry about. This van is a special-purpose vehicle. It can drown out any interference from the outside."

Chapter Two

The screeching sound of the van, as it hustled through the jungle more than an hour after leaving the highway, drowned the hushed whimpers coming from Tish and Jesse.

"How long before we get there?" Eli asked, trying his best to hold back tears of his own.

"If we continue our journey on the highway, we could get there in an hour forty-five minutes. This route will take a little longer. At least three more hours. We have to throw them off our track. That is why we're driving through the jungle."

"Three hours?" Jesse exclaimed. "Do we at least break at any point? Who are these people by the way? I mean, Tidal Tours, Love Experiment, what do they want with us?"

"Hold on!" they heard the driver yell as the van cranked to speed up a steep hill before roaring to life and landing on the other side with a thud. Everyone grabbed the seat in front of them as they struggled to regain their balance.

"Easy now!" Agent Drummonds yelled at the driver as Jesse let out a blood-curdling scream when they approached a narrow bridge. She covered her eyes with both hands and held her breath from fear that the van would plummet down to the rocks and get carried away, with them inside, by the churning river below.

The driver's eyes were fixed on the road, firmly holding the steering. At the other end of the bridge, he turned to maneuver a few more rough patches before he landed on a dirt road, traveling at seventy miles per hour.

Three hours turned into four, and then five. The van roared, stopping at intervals for bathroom breaks at the side of the road and occasionally to fill the gas tank from a can in the trunk.

"I thought this was a three-hour journey at most. It feels like we've been driving for what seems like an eternity." Adam said, sounding frustrated.

"We won't be much longer. Maybe one hour," Agent Drummonds responded.

"A whole hour?" Jesse groaned. "I can't take this anymore," she whispered to Eli.

"We've come this far my love. Try to wait this out for my sake. I'm sure we'll get there soon. It has to happen sometime," Eli responded, kissing her lightly on the forehead.

A delicious chill coursed through Jesse at the affection Eli had doled to her at that moment. If his behavior towards her in the past few days was anything to reckon with, she could heal from the trauma she'd suffered from this experience with him by her side. Though their present situation had been unwelcome and devastating, she felt she could live with it if it meant being as in love as she was now with Eli.

Snuggling closer, she placed her head on his chest, wrapped her hand around his waist, and whispered, "I love you too."

"I love you more than life itself," he responded, kissing her lightly on the head and squeezing her until she chuckled quietly.

Before long, they swerved through a sloping driveway. Within sight were the grounds of a large white house with windows on all sides and a balcony wrapping around the entire circumference as far as the eyes could see. As the car drove onto the porch, a sinewy man in his sixties opened the door and greeted them as they stepped out. He led them through a large lobby to an elevator up one floor, where each couple settled into their rooms.

"I forgot something important," Adam said after the door shut behind them.

"What?" Tish asked.

"I wanted to ask that agent a thing or two. We don't even know his station. Also, we should have asked him for replacement phones."

"We can go down now and look for him."

"Sure, let's," Adam said, taking Tish's hand in his and leading her out.

The sinewy man who showed them to their rooms was standing right outside their door, frowning when they stepped out. "Hey, you should be resting," he said, in a voice almost identical to his looks, dry, and thin.

"We just need to speak with agent Drummonds," Adam said.

"He has since left. What do you need?" the man said.

"We noticed there's no phone in the room. Do you have one? My girlfriend and I need to make a call. It's quite urgent."

"I don't think it's a good idea for you to make calls now, seeing that you're on a strict schedule," he muttered slowly. "Why don't you relax, take a shower, and prepare to have those chips removed."

"You know about that?" Tish asked, aghast.

"Yes, I do," the man answered. "Agent Drummonds left instructions. Once you finish with the procedure, you can call any place you want."

Adam nodded while Tish stared at the man in confusion. She was about to say something when Adam took her hand and walked right back into the room.

"Why was he tugging so much at his ear?" Tish asked the moment they closed the door behind them.

"Oh, you noticed that, too?" Adam responded, laughing. "That's strange."

"It feels as though he was getting fed word by word everything he said to us. You know, like in the movies," Tish added.

"Well, we could use some rest now. Agent Drummonds promised to contact the embassy tomorrow about our passports. We're in no desperate need of a phone now."

"I can't wait to go home," Tish said, kicking off her shoes. "And no matter how hard I try, I can't stop thinking about those other contestants. It's upsetting."

"Do you want to know what is even more upsetting?" Adam asked.

"I'm all ears," Tish said, sitting on the bed.

"I'd hinted something to you when you first woke up at the hospital. Since then, I've confirmed it with numerous examples."

"What exactly are you referring to?" Tish asked, tilting her head up and letting out a sigh.

"Since the heart transplant, I've noticed something odd. Do you remember that I've often accused you of being so particular, so meticulous?"

"I remember that vaguely," Tish responded, staring at him in anticipation. "Please, go on."

"Well, I think the tide has turned," Adam said. "I'm now all of those things I've accused you of. I feel like someone snuck up to me while I was sleeping at night and wound me up so tight."

"I'm still trying to figure out where you're going with this, Adam," Tish said, grimacing and shaking her head. "What do you mean by wound up tight?"

"I'm trying to say that I now behave like you."

"Like me?" Tish squealed, chuckling afterwards as she raised her legs and placed them on the bed as she continued to listen to Adam.

"You're not taking this seriously," Adam accused her.

"Why should I? It's funny that you imagine that I'm wound up tight. I never imagined myself to be like that. Yes, I take things too seriously sometimes, but to describe myself in those terms, I'll beg to differ."

"Okay, maybe not those words exactly," Adam said conceding defeat. "But I've noticed how laid back you've become, not hustling all the time like you used to. Being laid back is the kind of stuff I used to associate with myself. You were my exact opposite and I think that was why I was so attracted to you. Did you notice any changes in your temperament, or am I being ridiculous for thinking the exchange would have caused this?"

"Hmm, come to think of it," Tish said, nodding slowly. "The more you described the situation, I started to recall certain aspects of my behaviour that don't feel normal anymore. I remember you were alluding to that at the hospital, but it just didn't make any sense to me at that point. I'm starting to understand."

Adam hesitated for a second before responding. "I thought I was going crazy. I was so scared to bring it up with you.

"You're not crazy. I too have noticed a few things since this whole thing began. I feel like I've become more chilled. My old self would have been jumping up and down and screaming at everything in sight in our current predicament. I completely understand what you're trying to say."

"Thank God!" Adam exclaimed, kneeling before her on the bed and placing his head on her thighs. "Do you honestly agree?" he asked, raising his head to glance at her.

"I think so," Tish responded with a nod.

"Who would you rather be? Your old or new self?" Adam probed.

"Hands down, my new self."

"Really?"

"Without a doubt," Tish admitted gleefully. "But we can't help how we're created. Can we? As much as my heart tells me it does not belong to me, I can't help but be grateful that I don't have to worry so much ever again."

"Well, maybe that's part of what the experiment was supposed to achieve," Adam added. "Maybe by swapping our hearts, they swapped both our feelings and our personalities."

"Do you seriously believe that?" Tish asked, aghast.

"Is it not clear to you by now?"

"So, you believe this was their plan in making us go through this dangerous transformation? I don't believe that."

"Tish, the signs are in from of you. Remember when you started loving me?"

"Hmm," Tish muttered, tilting her head to the ceiling.

"Is it all making sense to you now? The same thing happened to Eli and Jesse. He told me that he was now deeply in love with Jesse."

"But they're married."

"Yes, but he confessed to me that they've been having problems and he hasn't loved her in a long time."

"No…no," Tish said, shaking her head. "There are so many factors that would cause him or even you and I to have a change of heart. Also, concerning the change in personality, there are many ways for one to change their mindset without getting cut, tortured, and bruised. I could have achieved the same goal by reorienting myself and changing how I approach things. Don't you think?"

"If that were true," Adam said, "don't you think I could revert to who I used to be by just changing my mindset? I remember that person. I cherish it, but somehow, I can't shake this new me."

"You seem so convinced this exchange changed you."

"With a hundred percent certainty," Adam said in a monotone.

"I'm not fully convinced, but if it's any consolation, I'll remind you that this new you could come in handy sometimes. Being a serious person has its benefits," Tish said, smiling to calm him down.

"That's not all though," Adam said. "Anytime I stop for a rest, these images fly around in my subconscious. They seem like memories of a different time and place, but these memories are not mine. I wonder if the exchange did that too. It's as though I'm watching a movie about someone else's life. It's always there…In my mind's eye. Could they be yours?"

"Wait a minute," Tish said, pushing Adam's head away. She flashed her mouth open, frozen to the spot after Adam revealed his experience about the memories to her.

Adam stared at her and waited a few seconds for her mouth to close. "Are you experiencing that too?"

"Oh my God! It's happening to me too," she exclaimed, clasping her hands over her mouth. "Do you think this is an after-effect of the exchange, too? Will it ever stop?"

"I don't know," Adam responded sullenly.

"But I don't want them."

"Are these memories bothering you?"

"Yes…yes. I thought they were nightmares, but I just realized it could be something else."

"Do you mind sharing what you see?"

Tish grunted and shook her head. "Oh no, Adam. I'd rather not at this time."

"Why not? They're probably mine."

"What if they're not? What if the hospital lied to us? What if the hearts we received are from other people?" she said, pressing her hand firmly against her chest to control its heaving as she fixed Adam with a piercing stare. "What if everyone is lying to us?"

The more Tish spoke, the more the thought crossed her mind that she may be going through something more sinister than she had been led to believe. Her shoulders shook as she sobbed, at first quietly and then hysterically as Adam sat beside her and took her hand.

"I can't believe I'm saying this Tish, but we're going to be okay."

"What if…What if…All I know is that I want my own heart back."

"It'll be nice to get our original hearts back, but I think after all we've been through, surviving the surgery and all, we're lucky to have made it out alive. The other unfortunate contestants will give everything to trade places with us. Let's hold onto what we have right now. We may have to hold onto it for the rest of our lives, but it's better than being six feet under. It's also gotten us closer. To be honest, I'm so scared of losing it all. I'm so scared of losing you."

Tish looked into his eyes as though searching his soul for answers. "Really?" she muttered.

"I cross my heart," Adam said, making a sign of the cross.

"I'm scared of losing you, too," Tish said, placing her head on his shoulder as she wiped her face with the back of her hand.

"Say that again," Adam prodded.

"I'm scared of losing you," she repeated, "but the only thing I want to do now is go home."

Chapter Three

Eli and Jesse were facing a different challenge of their own.

"Don't freak out," Eli whispered to Jesse as soon as she kicked off her shoes to relax on the bed. "I noticed something on the way to our room that tells me something is seriously wrong with our decision to follow Agent Drummonds and his men here."

"You know I'm going to freak out when you ask me not to," Jesse replied, fixing her eyes on him.

"Did you notice the tattoo on that man's neck?" Eli asked.

Jesse shrugged and shook her head in confusion. In her exhaustion, she had barely looked at the man who brought them to their room, let alone noticed something as inconsequential as a tattoo.

"I've seen that mark before," Eli continued. "The tour agent in Boston had the same tattoo at the same spot on her neck the day I went to sign the contracts. It's an echoing heart with an arrow piercing through it."

"Is this a joke?" Jesse said, immediately sitting upright.

"It might just be a coincidence," Eli said after a second's pause. "If it—" Eli began to say and was halted by a knock on the door.

Agent Drummonds walked into the room with a stern look on his face before they could answer the door.

"I thought you'd be sleeping after that long drive," he said gruffly. "You should rest before your operation to remove the chips tonight."

"Operation?" Eli asked. "I thought we were to undergo a minor procedure."

"That's what it is, but we don't know exactly where they inserted the chip so it may take a while. Just make sure you have nothing to eat after eight. The operation is at ten."

"Are we going to be put under? Will a qualified doctor be handling this?" Eli asked.

Agent Drummonds tugged at the bottom of his shirt as Eli spoke. "Yes. A qualified doctor will be taking care of you."

As he rubbed the back of his head when he turned to leave, Jesse spotted the tattoo Eli had described earlier at the base of Agent Drummonds' neck but waited for him to shut the door before whispering, "Did you see that, Eli?"

"I did!" Eli's heart was racing as he tried to catch his breath. The fear was evident on his face, as it had turned a bright shade of red. He grabbed onto the door handle, trying to get a grip on reality in the midst of the chaos. "We have to get out of here now," he said, his voice shaking with panic. The urgency of the situation was clear, and it only added to the already tense atmosphere.

"How?" Jesse mumbled. "We drove for over six hours to get to this location. We don't have any phones. We don't have passports. We don't even have any money. These people were supposed to take care of all that."

She looked panic-stricken and failed to see Eli putting his index finger on his mouth to urge her to quiet down.

"Calm down Jesse," he whispered, grabbing her hands. "If these people are who we think they are, they're probably watching us and overhearing everything we say." He walked stealthily to the door and noticed it did not have a proper lock. He then roamed the room searching for cameras and any spying devices, but there were no visible ones.

Jesse rose from the bed and squeezed his hands as though her life depended on it. "We have to find a way to alert Adam and Tish," she whispered.

"What if they're in on this?"

"That's impossible. How can you say that? We can't leave without them."

"Jesse, we can't trust anyone at this time. What if these so-called friends have been tricking us this whole time?"

"I doubt it. I saw Adam's scar with my own eyes. They've been with us through this entire ordeal. We can't abandon them now. If these 'love' people were to make any of us undergo additional procedures, we may not make it out alive. I can't believe we drove this far into the jungle with them. We don't even know where we are. For all you know, we've left Costa Rica and landed in Panama or Nicaragua."

"We don't have time to figure that out now. Let's go," he urged her.

———————————

They walked out of the room, hand in hand, into Tish and Adam's room, without as much as a knock to warn them. Eli couldn't believe the turn of events and it left him feeling helpless. But he knew he had to stay strong for himself and for Jesse.

"Hey guys," Adam began to say, stunned by their sudden reappearance. He stopped after Eli placed one finger on his lips and beckoned them to the direction of the balcony.

When they were all gathered on the balcony, Eli and Jesse, whispering and gesturing quietly, revealed all they knew.

"We need to act fast," Adam said, a look of alarm registered all over his face.

"What exactly should we do?" Tish said frantically.

"We keep moving and hope for the best," Eli said. "Whatever we do, we cannot allow them to place us under their control again. If the need arises, we should fight with our bare hands since we have no weapons."

With nothing more than the clothes on their back, they snuck past the hallway and down a flight of stairs. They headed to the foyer without a concrete plan except to steal the van and keep driving until they were out of danger. Their escape progressed without incident until they stepped onto the porch, and a piercing sound blasted their ears, causing them to run in the direction of the bushes, abandoning their quest. Six armed men rushed towards them as they scuttled further away, but they were no match for their pursuers. Being in unfamiliar surroundings, they ran haphazardly, in no particular direction, with alarm on their faces. The men rounded them and yanked them back into the mansion. Tish continued to kick and scream while Jesse stayed surprisingly still, though the terror she felt at that moment showed in her eyes. Adam and Eli were both flanked by two guards. The men dragged them into a padded room, further restraining them by forcing their hands behind their backs.

"Let go," My chest is hurting," Tish cried.

"You'll not get away with this," Eli assured their captors in a cool tone. "Let us go now, and we'll forget this ever happened."

"We have no plans to hurt you," one of the men said. "You'll be released as soon as you calm down."

As they were pleading with the guards, two men in long white coats entered the room, marched to Eli and Adam, and inserted syringes into their arms. Panic set in as they realized they were being drugged, but it was too late. The drugs burned in their veins, the world spinning out of control. Tish and Jesse stared in confusion. They were forced to their knees, their bodies struggling against the overwhelming strength of their assailants before the world went dark and their consciousness faded away.

Chapter Four

Eli regained consciousness on the third day. Without food or drink to sustain him, and the drugs still wreaking havoc in his system, he stumbled a few times as he rose from the bed. By his fifth try, the rustle of a key on the door startled him, so he hurriedly lay back down, pulling the sheets over his shoulders. A bulky man in a white uniform and thick lens walked in with a tray. He forced a smile and nodded before muttering something in Spanish. As he turned to place the contents of the tray on the desk, Eli crept behind him and bashed his head on the wall. The man fell instantly, hitting his head on the desk on the way down. Knocked out cold, his hands and legs sprawled in every direction. Eli repeatedly kicked his hand to confirm he was unconscious before kneeling beside him and searching his pockets one after the other until he found a wallet and a set of keys on a ring. He stuffed those in his underwear and rolled the man on his back to collect the pistol he had seen lodged in a holster on his waist before quietly sneaking out. Outside the room was a deserted hallway with large window screens and a massive glass chandelier hanging from high ceilings, illuminating the whole space. A flight of stairs led him down to the next floor, where two rooms faced each other on either side of the landing. "Thank God," he muttered under his breath as the door to the first room flung open when he tried the keys. He saw Jesse lying on the narrow bed, moving her legs slowly as the effects of the drugs were beginning to wear off. Without hesitation, he dashed to her side and leaned over.

"Jesse," he whispered.

"Hmm," she mumbled as she tried to open her eyes.

"Shh," Eli warned, placing a finger on her lips.

Still unaware of her surroundings, she began to squeal and writhe uncontrollably prompting Eli to clasp his hand firmly around her mouth, pushing her head into the pillow to force her to stop. She opened her eyes fully at that moment, startled at first before a twinkle appeared in them when she recognized Eli. Eli slowly released his hold and pulled her close for a hug.

"My love," she whispered, sobbing as she kissed his lips.

"You have to work with me to get us out of here," he said with a sense of urgency, helping her to her feet. "Can you use your legs?

"I'm not sure. I could try."

"What is this?" he asked as her feet touched the ground, and he noticed the round red spot on her right leg.

"I don't know," she said, casting him a bewildered gaze.

"What on earth is going on here?" he screeched after he pulled up his pant leg and noticed a bruise in the same spot as Jesse's on his leg.

At the sight of Eli's bruise, Jesse slumped and fell on the floor. His was larger, more protruded, and had begun to turn blue at the corners. It became clear to Eli then that the people they had trusted to save them had subdued and subjected them to another medical procedure — another sign that something more sinister was brewing. With his newly sharpened intuition, he felt convinced they were being held captive by monsters.

"Jesse my love," he whispered, bending to lift her off the floor.

"I…I need to throw up," she mumbled.

"Go ahead if that will make you feel better," he said, holding her head up. As nothing came up, he held her firmly by the waist and slowly led her out of the room. "We need to find Adam and Tish," he continued, placing her gently on the stairs. "Wait here while I go look for them."

"This is going to be harder than I thought," Eli grunted when none of the keys could open the door across from Jesse's.

"Maybe there are rooms downstairs," Jesse suggested.

"There are also rooms upstairs. Wait, let me check the upper floor!"

He trotted up the stairs, past his room and another flight of stairs, until he arrived at the penthouse. His heart pounded as the door flung open on the first try. Adam and Tish were awake in the two adjoining rooms.

Tish recoiled when she saw him. Besides everything that was going on, she seemed overly agitated, shrinking her body, and retreating to the end of the bed. He walked by her to get to Adam. "Is she okay?" he asked.

"Eli, we don't know what to think anymore," Adam stated. "Everywhere…Every step we take, we always seem to head right back to where we started or even worse."

"I know, but we don't have time. Jesse is waiting downstairs. You need to hurry. We must leave now," Eli demanded, his hand gestures pleading with them to stay calm.

How did you get that?" Adam asked, pointing to the pistol Eli was waving around.

"Oh!" he muttered, taking one look at the gun and hiding it in his waist. He had not realized he was holding it menacingly. "From the guard…For protection. We need to leave. I believe the coast is clear now. Come with me," he ordered, waving his hands.

They converged on Jesse's floor and walked down another flight of stairs to the foyer. It seemed clear for a moment, but just as they were about to step out on the porch, four guards charged toward them and pointed rifles directly at their heads.

Staring at one another in horror, they scuttled to the stairs.

"Stop, or we'll shoot," one of the men roared, raising his gun and firing above their heads. Jesse screamed at the deafening sound. White plaster rained down from the ceiling, where the bullet had formed a gaping hole.

"Keep going," Eli muttered, forcing Adam, Tish, and Jesse out of shock, and leading them up the stairs, but they were still no match for the guards, who, within seconds, rounded them up and forced them to the ground.

"Don't hurt us," Adam pleaded. "We'll do whatever you want. Please."

Eli tried to reach for the pistol he had hidden in his pants, but it dropped to the ground and made a loud thud that distracted his assailant. While the man was trying to figure out the source of the sound, Eli scrambled to his feet and kicked the guard on his knee pit, causing the man to groan and fall to his knees, but before Eli could reach for his pistol, the guard recovered and got on his feet.

"Backup," the guard roared as Eli dodged his menacing fist and jabbed him in the chest. With his medium build, the guard was no match for Eli, who delivered another punch before another guard sprinted down the stairs and forced Eli's face to the floor. As he lay there, the first man struck his head with the base of his gun. He did it with such intensity the sound could be heard all over the foyer, like the splintering of wood. Eli moaned as warm blood ran down his ear, and he struggled to free himself from their grip.

"You'll kill him," Jesse screamed, tears rolling down her cheeks, her chest heaving. She tried to stand and go to him, but her captor pushed her shoulder firmly so she could not move from her position. Her eyes darted from person to person as she twisted and turned to free herself. When her efforts failed, she started to berate the men.

"Leave us alone. Haven't you done enough?" she reprimanded.

"Shut your mouth," the first man yelled.

"Help… Help!" Jesse started to scream at the top of her lungs without fear of repercussions as she started believing they were more valuable to their captors alive and well, than dead or injured.

Tish joined in the effort and screamed for help, but each time they opened their mouths, the men tightened their grip on their arms.

"You should be ashamed of yourselves," Adam said when he realized what they were doing to the women. "You'll pay for this. That's a promise."

Chapter Five

They had lost all hope of escape when one of the assailants yelled, "We have company," as the guards yanked them off their feet and led them up the stairs.

At first, it sounded like an airplane droning in the distance until they realized a helicopter was heading in their direction. It hovered noisily outside, wielding a siren as loud as a fire truck. Bright lights flashed onto the foyer, blinding everyone in sight. The ground shook. The lights slowly dimmed so they could make out a fleet of police vehicles and uniformed policemen strategically positioned with their weapons, calmly waiting for instructions to act as a voice from a loudspeaker announced, "Free the prisoners… I say, free the prisoners!"

The guards could see they were outnumbered and obeyed the order by slowly letting go of their kidnapped victims and dropping their guns on the ground.

"Place your hands over your heads and file out in a single line," another order stated.

The guards looked at one another and did as they were told. The policemen quickly rounded them up and placed metal handcuffs on them before shoving them one at a time at the back of two police cars.

Eli and the others froze to the spot. After all the trauma they'd endured, they were now mere shadows of their former selves. They stood in their positions for instructions or a cue for what to do next. Two policemen marched in, and one after the other led them outside, starting with Eli, followed by Adam, and then Jesse. Before they could get to Tish, Agent Drummonds appeared from nowhere, crept behind her, and clasped his hand around her middle. Shielding his body with hers, he pointed a gun directly at her head.

"Hostage situation," the voice from the loudspeaker announced as Agent Drummonds slowly strode back, his hand grabbing Tish more firmly as she gasped for breath and clawed at him with both hands.

"Still, or I'll shoot," he growled into her ear.

Tish froze and allowed him to lead her in whatever direction he pleased.

"What are your demands?" the voice from the loudspeaker asked.

"Release my men. I'll count till ten, and if I don't see them in the foyer, I'll blow her head off," Agent Drummonds responded while still retreating.

"We will release one of your men," the voice on the loudspeaker said.

"All six men or we have no deal," Agent Drummonds retorted and began counting, "One… Two… Three," continuing his retreat. Adam charged twice in a dangerous attempt to offer himself in exchange for Tish, but two policemen bound him by the hands.

"You're wasting your time, Adam. I have the person I want," Agent Drummonds sneered loudly.

"Coward!" Adam called.

It was clear to everyone why Tish was his target. With her small size, she was easy bait. Adam would be harder to restrain.

"Four…," Agent Drummonds continued, ignoring his insult.

He took another step backward and tripped against a stair, staggering, and accidentally pushing the gun firmly against Tish's head.

She let out a blood-curdling scream, trembling, eyes round with fear.

"Shut your mouth. Consider yourself lucky to be breathing. Five…" He was yelling at the top of his voice, shaking feverishly as he spoke. The beads of sweat that had collected on his forehead started to drip down his lids, blurring his vision. When he released the gun from her head to wipe his eye with the back of his hand, Tish saw her chance and elbowed him in the groin. The cracking sound of a gun went off, and she fell to the ground clutching her right cheek, a scream escaping her lips. A second gunshot could be heard from a distance, and Agent Drummonds fell on his knees beside Tish, his gun clattering to the ground. Blood splattered all over the floor around Tish, and even more blood gushed out of Agent Drummonds' neck. One of the policemen had shot him. Tish quivered as Adam and Eli clamored towards her.

"Come with us," the voice of a policeman boomed from behind. Another wrapped a bandage around Agent Drummonds' neck to control the bleeding. Despite his racing pulse and panic-filled eyes, he was amazingly calm as two policemen dragged him onto the porch.

Another policeman dashed into the foyer and carried Tish out, placing her at the back of a police car and administering first aid.

Adam ran to Tish.

"It's only a flesh wound," the policeman assured him. "I've put a Band-Aid on it. Once the bleeding stops, she'll be fine."

"How do you know?" Jesse asked.

"I've checked it. He just grazed her cheek. If he had meant to kill her, trust me, he would have succeeded," the policeman insisted, glaring at him.

"Thank God," Adam said, kneeling beside Tish. He held her chin to check the wound. "I was so scared this madman would kill you.

Tish, still visibly shaken, held Adam's head with both hands and kissed him.

"We need to leave," one of the policemen alerted them. "Please head to that van. A doctor will check you really quick before we move."

"Who are you?" Adam asked.

"FBI."

Adam shook his head. "So, who was that guy? The one that called himself agent Drummonds."

"An impersonator…I'm sure you've realized that by now. Hurry, we have to leave right away," he said, marching them to the van.

Chapter Six

The expressionless doctor that appeared at the door of the full-size van was firm. "You can finish later," he said to Jesse and Eli, who immediately stopped kissing and caressing at the sound of his voice. They thanked him as he held each of their hands to let them inside and offered them seats in the space behind the driver. He started by examining the cut on Eli's leg.

"How bad is it, doctor?" Eli asked, looking down when he saw the alarm on the doctor's face.

"I'm sorry for what you've all been through," the doctor said, pushing Eli's head back up. "You look like you've been to hell and back. How did you get this?"

"We all have a similar bruise on our legs. I'd like to believe they removed a chip, but only God knows what happened."

"I don't think anything was removed," the doctor said, strapping a sphygmomanometer to Eli's hand before placing a thermometer under his tongue. "The situation seems to be the opposite. There's a subdermal implant somewhere there. It could be a chip or something else. You'll have to wait till we get you to a proper hospital to have whatever was inserted in there located and extracted."

After Eli, he examined Jesse and then Adam, and for each one of them, he came to the same dire conclusion that their captors had implanted a device under the pretext of removing imaginary chips.

When he got to Tish, he asked her to lie on a bench. "Your temperature is rising alarmingly," he said, raising her shirt and running his hand across her scar. "It's healed nicely, though."

"So, what could be the issue," Adam asked, a look of terror spreading across his face.

"Nothing life-threatening, I hope. I'll give her something to control the fever, but she needs to get to a hospital as soon as possible so they can run some tests. You all need immediate medical attention. Consider yourselves lucky to have come out of this alive. Not many would have survived this."

"What do you know?" Adam's tone was pleading.

As Adam was waiting for him to respond, the doctor reached for a duffle bag, took out four pairs of linen pants and t-shirts, and handed one to each of them as they anxiously waited for his response to Adam's question.

"From what I've heard, Tidal Tours and the Love Experiment are a front for a crime ring that is involved in extensive illegal medical research for a breakthrough in how people meet and fall in love. As you can imagine, such an accomplishment will change the way the world operates and create fortunes. With almost eight billion people on earth, this endeavor is extremely lucrative as everyone craves love in one way or the other. These people don't care that they're cheating nature and playing God. They lure unsuspecting romantics like you, swap your hearts, and monitor as you fall in and out of love so they can achieve their goal."

"Why did they target us?" Eli asked.

"I don't know. That's something you'd have to figure out for yourselves or better still, wait till the FBI completes their investigation. All I know is that you're not the first. This has been going on for a few years, and there have been multiple casualties. The FBI has been hot on their trail even though yours is the first breakthrough in this case. This ring uses its victims as guinea pigs in an experiment that in the future may not necessarily involve heart transplants but rather will rely on the concept that traces of memories are retained in cell bodies, so they can manipulate the way people fall in and out of love."

Adam and Eli looked at each other and shook their heads in disappointment.

"Have you noticed any changes in the way your mind processes feelings and memories?" the doctor continued.

Their eyes met and they shared a knowing look, silently acknowledging the confusion between them. Each nod was deliberate and slow, signifying their understanding without the need for words.

"I've noticed thoughts that are not mine and dreams that belong to another person. Maybe they're Tish's. I don't know," Adam finally said, shrugging. "I love Tish, but I can do without memories that don't belong to me. Her memories bother her, too, and I feel so stupid for getting both of us into this predicament."

"Do you feel you love her more now than you did before?" the doctor asked.

"Pretty much," he responded, looking deeply into Tish's eyes. "I love her more than I can ever love anything in this world. I love her more than life itself."

Tish's eyes glazed as she let out a deep sigh. She turned away, wrapping her blanket tightly around her for comfort. Her vision blurred as she tried to hold back the tears, lost in her own thoughts. The sight of her hunched figure, disoriented and vulnerable, tugged at Adam's heartstrings.

"Seemed they achieved their purpose then," the doctor declared after witnessing their emotional exchange.

"I believe so," Adam confirmed, shooting Tish a glance as she wiped the tears off her face.

"There's one more thing I'd like to share with you," the doctor continued. "The tour company traps all these couples but only transplants some. They sometimes maintain a control group amongst their conquests. This group received placebos—"

"What does that mean?" Jesse asked while the others looked around in horror.

"It means some of the victims go through the same process as someone who received a heart transplant. They get the cuts, the bruises, the whole nine yards, and retain their own hearts, having not undergone any transplant at all."

"This is out of hand!" Jesse exclaimed, her lower lip quivering. "I don't know whether to be happy or sad about this. All I know is that these people should get the punishment they deserve."

"I need to clarify something," Adam interjected, wide-eyed. "So, basically, other than not knowing with a hundred percent certainty the heart we received, we may also not have been transplanted at all?"

"Correct," the doctor responded, nodding. "Only the surgeon knows who he transplanted. The tour company obtains this information from the doctors and uses the chips they implant in their victims to monitor their every move. These couples don't know what hit them because, on the day of the surgeries, they are drugged and out of it. I must add that I'm shocked by the scars I see on your chests. In a few of the past cases, they completed these transplants with state-of-the-art equipment that left very little scaring, so the victims never discovered what happened to them until they started experiencing other symptoms. I can't explain how they achieved that feat. It's still a mystery to me and my colleagues. They must have been low on options in your case to have made these hideous cuts on you. Despite that, I still maintain you're lucky to be alive. As you know, four others in your batch died in this process."

All four of them were astonished for a while as the doctor organized his tools in his bag. Eli, who had been too shocked to speak since the doctor's recent declaration finally mustered the strength to say something. Chuckling awkwardly, he said, "So, this was a psychological experiment gone wrong."

"Seems like it," the doctor said. "Unfortunately you and your friends paid the prize. I guess you thought you were dealing with a legitimate tour company. You have to be careful next time. Don't accept everything that dangles its tail in front of you."

"We were fooled," Eli said.

"I'm so sorry, Eli," Jesse whispered. "I should have known it sounded too good to be true. I thought we were getting the chance to enjoy an all-expense paid trip somewhere warm. I would have never thought in a million years we would be pawns in a radical experiment…"

"Until it was too late to escape?" Eli helped her finish as she started sobbing halfway through her speech. "Nothing in life is free," he muttered, gently grabbing her waist and kissing her forehead. "I've always known that, so I only have myself to blame for this predicament."

"I've completed my examination," the doctor announced, smiling dryly as he interrupted their intimate moment. "You're all now in stable condition. The police escorts will take you to a safe location where you'll spend the night and leave for the States tomorrow. Take care of yourselves. I hope you recover from your physical and emotional wounds soon."

Chapter Seven

It was already dusk when they arrived at the airfield, where two men transferred them to a small plane. Bright orange lights leaked through the trees, and the setting sun marked an end to their ordeal. As the engines whirred, the police cars retreated in a single file to return to their stations, heading east and raising so much dust behind them. A little after take-off, a tall, lean man wearing a face cap with an abstract logo appeared from the cockpit and greeted them warmly before shouting instructions to the pilot.

Eli noticed something oddly familiar about the man as he approached them. "It's Ty," he screeched, causing all four of them to run towards the door, banging and screaming at the top of their lungs, hoping someone would rescue them. The last of the police cars had since left, and they were several feet above the ground, so they felt caught between the devil and the deep blue sea, having to choose between jumping from the plane or collectively tackling Ty.

"Hey man, we don't want any trouble," Adam pleaded when he came to his senses. "What do you want with us?"

"Calm down," Ty said, gesturing with both hands. "I'm not the enemy. Look," he continued, reaching into his breast pocket to pull out a badge and an ID. "I'm special agent Dylan Sundry."

"Ty…And now, Dylan. Prove it!" Jesse demanded.

"I've shown you my badge and ID. How else do you want me to prove that I'm telling you the truth? You know me as Ty, but I've been working undercover for two years to apprehend these criminals. Please sit down and I'll explain everything to you."

Without much choice left in the matter, Tish and Jesse slowly took their seats, while Adam and Eli waited by the door with bated breath.

"We stumbled on the perfect opportunity when we found out they were looking for tour agents," Ty continued. "I applied to join the team as the position was paramount for keeping track of the victims. This is the closest we'd ever come to catching these monsters. They were constantly monitoring us, so I had to be careful. Our original plan was to secure your lodgings, so we could capture the culprits before they did any real harm, but they accomplished their goal before we were able to complete our mission. Who do you think called 911?"

"You're the mystery caller?" Jesse mumbled.

Ty nodded.

"Why didn't you answer when we called you?" Tish interjected.

"I could not say anything to you that would give away the plan, and by the time they transferred you to the hospital, it was too late. These people's work is so far-reaching they can pay off any hospital to take their cases. I don't expect you to believe right away that I'm not one of them, but eventually, you'll have to."

"We don't know what to believe anymore," Eli answered, taking his seat when he saw Adam do the same. "We have been lied to, cheated, abused, and butchered. I think I'd be speaking for everyone if I say we're the wrong people to ask that question."

"Why didn't you rescue us from the bungalow?" Tish asked. "You waited for us to undergo additional torture before you finally came. Didn't you know they moved us there?"

"We could have taken you from the hospital, but you were too sick to move. The agent we planted amongst the staff informed us about your move to the bungalow. We had planned to rescue you from there, but when they got wind of it, they moved you before we could get to you."

"How did you finally find us?" Tish asked.

"It was rough, but I refused to budge even though it proved to be the most difficult case. We were lucky in the end."

"How exactly?" Adam asked.

Ty retreated into the cockpit and returned some seconds later with a few sheets of paper, which he distributed to them. "Recognize yourselves in these?" he asked.

"The photos!" Tish exclaimed.

"Seems you've seen these before."

"Of course," Tish squealed. "Agent Drummonds showed them to us the day he claimed to be rescuing us.

"The day you were moved from the bungalow, they attacked an agent of ours who had taken pictures of you to send to the embassy. Although he managed to escape, he did not leave the vicinity as he feared time was of the essence, and he was right. When he saw the man you know as 'Agent Drummonds' at your door, he snuck under the vehicle without their knowing and placed a tracking device on the undercarriage. This was how we were able to track you."

"I guess we should thank you for saving our lives," Tish said, eliciting surprise stares from Eli and Jesse.

"You're welcome. I was just doing my job," Ty muttered, taking the seat in front. "Your passports and travel documents are ready. You'll stay in a hotel in San Jose tonight and leave for the States tomorrow."

When they arrived at the hotel, they got the chance to speak to their families on the phone for the first time in days, leaving everyone in awe of what to expect when they finally reunited. Not knowing who amongst them was carrying another's heart or who was a walking placebo, they became skeptical about the bonds they had formed — bonds that could last forever or get destroyed with the changes in their bodies. Despite all their concerns, most especially having monitoring chips still implanted in their bodies, all that mattered then was to get home.

Acknowledgments

First, I would like to thank the Almighty God, the source of my inspiration and without whom everything would be nothing.

Writing a novel is a very lonely exercise, so when I emerge from my cocoon, I feel blessed to be surrounded by people I admire.

Massive love and appreciation for my family and friends. You have been there from the beginning, supporting and encouraging me.

To my beta readers, Ogbo, Kene, Dumkele, Nnamdi, and Ogo, I greatly appreciate you giving me the gift of your time to read my drafts. Your advice and feedback really helped me take the story to new levels.

To my editor, publicist, virtual assistants, and graphic designers, thank you for your help and guidance through this process. You made the load lighter.

Finally, a huge thank-you to my readers. You make me feel that the massive effort involved in writing and publishing a book is worth its while.

Also by Oby Aligwekwe

NFUDU: Skirts, Ties & Taboos

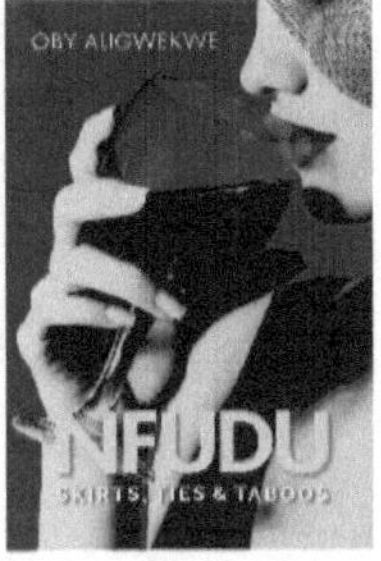

Praise for NFUDU

"A Delicious Read" – KC M, London, UK

"A Heart Tugging Story" – Juliet, Canada

"Very educative, with lots of history interwoven with romance, and filled with suspense and crazy twists that took my breath away." – Chikaego, U.S

Hazel House

Praise for Hazel House

"Nail-biting suspense with twists and turns, not knowing whodunnit until the very end." – Lena, Canada

"A must read for lovers of murder mysteries and romance, with enough suspense, intrigues, twists and turns to keep you on the edge to the very last page." – Ifey, US

The Place Beyond Her Dreams

Praise for The Place Beyond Her Dreams

"Young adults and older readers will be enchanted by this fantasy's magic, romance, and life lessons." — Booklife by Publishers Weekly

"Young adults ages 13 and up will find The Place Beyond Her Dreams an inviting, thought-provoking adventure that surveys family, communities, and the power and consequences of personal decisions." — D. Donovan, Senior Reviewer, Midwest Book Review

About The Author

Photos by Mina © 2022

Oby Aligwekwe is the award-winning author of Nfudu, Hazel House, The Place Beyond Her Dreams, and the Take Me Home Now psychological thriller series.

When Oby is not writing, she enjoys traveling to exotic locations and bringing pieces of her travel with her. She lives in Ontario with her family and supports her community through her charity Éclat Beginnings.

Twitter: obyaligwekwe
Facebook: obyaligwekweauthor
Instagram: obyaligwekwe
Tiktok: obyaligwekwe_author
Website: www.obyaligwekwe.com